A

Charming

Crime

A Magical Cure Mystery

Dedication and Acknowledgments

I want to thank every single member of the Tonya Kappes Street Team! They are a group of readers who have stood by me and supported me. Readers are so important to me and I'm honored that at the end of the day they take the time to escape into my imaginative world. You guys rock!! AND I love you to death!

Thanks to reader, Ann Miller, for winning the Name My Magical Village Contest in the Magical Cures Series! Whispering Falls is the perfect name!

A big huge thanks to Eddy, Jack, Austin, and Brady (my guys!) for giving the reassurance to follow my dreams and supporting me throughout our day!

Edition: June 2012

Copyright © 2012 by Tonya Kappes

All rights reserved

Cover Artist: Laura Morrigan

www.lauramorrigan.com

License Notes

ISBN-13: 978-1477594520

ISBN-10: 1477594523

What others are saying about Author Tonya Kappes

"Full of wit, humor and colorful characters, Tonya Kappes delivers a fun, fast-paced story that will leave you hooked!" Bestselling Author, Jane Porter

"Fun, fresh, and flirty, Carpe Bead 'Em is the perfect read on a hot summer day. Tonya Kappes' voice shines in her debut novel." Author Heather Webber

"Tonya Kappes strings together the perfect blend of family, friends, and fun." Author Misa Ramirez

"I loved how Tonya Kappes was able to bring her characters to life." Coffee Table Reviews

"I love, love, love this book. I enjoyed reading about Hallie's friendships and her trials and tribulations. Her Aunt Grace was a hoot, especially the pink poodle. Too darn funny. As you already know I was crying and I had to put the book down. That, makes a truly awesome read for me, because I became a part of the story and loved Aunt Grace as much as Hallie.

Again, this was worth the wait and I can't wait to read your next story." Reader, Dru Ann

"I don't write many reviews but some books are so outstanding I just have to. This is one of them. Tonya Kappes is one of the freshest new voices in women's fiction, and I can't wait to read more from her." Reader, Melissa Lapierre

"This book was fun, entertaining and good to the last page. Who knew reading auras could get Olivia in so much trouble? Sit back, smile and cozy up to Splitsville.com, where Olivia does the dumping for you. There's heap loads of humor, a dose of magical realism, sprinkles of romance, and mystery when someone ends up dead!" Author Lisa Lim

"This book was funny and clever with a unique premise. I truly couldn't put it down." Author Diane Majeske

"Tonya Kappes has written a fast paced cozy mystery that kept me guessing till the end. Full of likeable characters, Splitsville.com is humerous and I was caught up in the story right from the beginning. I'm definitely looking forward to more books in this series!" Author Sheila Seabrook

"Unique, imaginative, funny, with a tantalizing mystery to boot. What more could one ask. But there was more ... compassion and passion ... Olivia is an animal lover with the good sense not to become jaded by her "day job" of helping people break up. She gets the guy, solves the puzzle and rises above all of life's messy situations. Aunt Matilda was the icing on the cake ... as I said ... PURE MAGIC." Reader PJ Schott

"I loved this book. Grandberry Falls is my kind of town and I for one would love to live there and get to know all the local folks. I enjoyed reading this book and can't wait to read the next book about Grandberry Falls by Tonya Kappes. I have added Tonya Kappes as one of my new favorite authors." Jean Segal

"I love it when I pick up a book because of its cover and the story to follow is just as great or better. That's what happened here." Stephanie Overton

"I read this in a day and loved it! You felt that you were part of Grandberry Falls. The small town folks who know everyone and know everything about someone in a matter of hours." Avid Reader

"I was looking for something different and easy to read...meaning nothing too involved, something that if I put down could come back to and remember all the characters and where I left off at...well I didn't put it down I finished it in a day... what a great read !!" Cimarron

Also by Tonya Kappes

Women's Fiction

Carpe Bead 'em

Anthologies

Something Spooky This Way Comes

Believe Christmas Anthology

Olivia Davis Paranormal Mystery Series

Splitsville.com (Book One)

Magical Cures Mystery Series

A Charming Crime

Grandberry Falls Series

The Ladybug Jinx

Happy New Life

A Superstitious Christmas

Never Tell Your Dreams

A Divorced Diva Beading Mystery Series

A Bead of Doubt

Chapter One

"I know, I know." I waved my hands in front of me trying to stop anything that was about to come out of Oscar Park's mouth, but I knew it was useless.

He slammed the door of his patrol car, took his hat off, and then waved it towards my shed. . .my burning shed. "You know what?"

Truth be told, I didn't know much, but I did know how to handle Oscar Park. Especially when it came to personal matters. "I know I went a bit too far this time, but I really need to figure out this new cure."

Oscar grew up across the street, raised by his uncle, Police Chief Jordan Parks. Like me, well sort of like me, Oscar's parents got killed in a car accident while my dad was shot in the line of duty.

"A bit?" Oscar shook his head and pointed to the flames shooting up in the air. "Unless you want the new cure to blow someone up, I think you were using the wrong ingredients."

"Now, Oscar." I shuffled out of the way of the zipping fire truck, and took a bite of the Ding Dong in my hand that I had grabbed on the way out of the shed when I knew it was going to combust. "Was it necessary to call in all of Locust Grove's finest?"

"Yes, June Heal." Oscar wasn't the ten-year-old boy who created havoc with me in that very shed while experimenting with my mom Darla's homeopathic cures. Though his crystal blue eyes were sincere, I knew he meant business. "But you've done it this time. It's a total loss."

I held the uneaten round end of the Ding Dong up to him and he took a bite. A big bite. I grumbled under my breath. He knew Ding Dongs are my go-to comfort food.

Old Mac McGurtle came running through the herb garden I had planted after Darla died, screaming, "I told you she was going to set this whole town on fire if she kept mixing those chemicals."

Mr. McGurtle was always spreading gossip when Darla died about how I had turned A Dose of Darla, my homeopathic cure shop, into a fire hazard by putting all sorts of crazy concoctions together.

"Settle down, Mr. McGurtle." Jordan Parks snuck up behind us. "Thank you for calling us, and helping Ms. Heal save her business."

"Hhmph." Mr. McGurtle threw his hands in the air and mumbled something under his breath.

"He's the one who called?" I huffed, my bangs flew out of my eyes, and I crossed my arms. "He needs to mind his own business. And stop walking through my herb garden!"

For a moment Mr. McGurtle and I stared at each other until Jordan stepped between us.

The shed looked like it was going to be a total loss this time. All the other twenty times I set it afire I was able to save it. Luckily, I only used the shed to create new homeopathic cures using Darla's old remedies. I kept the main ingredients in the basement of our old house. . .my house now.

"I think you did it this time," Jordan warned, half serious. He walked away shaking his head. He stopped briefly to talk to one of the guys from the fire department.

"Not only have you done it this time, you've really pissed off a lot of your neighbors." Oscar put his hat back on his head, and looked around at the neighbors gathering on the other side of the fence in my front yard. "They think you are as crazy as Darla was."

Darla Heal, my mother, was the creator of A Dose of Darla, homeopathic cures. And everyone called her Darla, even me, because she didn't like to be referred to as Ms. Heal, Mrs. Heal or even Mom.

"Well, the old saying is right then." I snarled, studying every face gawking at me. They were just being nosy like always.

"And what old saying it that?" Oscar asked.

"The apple," I pointed to myself, "doesn't fall too far from the tree."

Oscar's face split into a wide grin. "And we sure did have some fun times in there. But you've got to admit you've outgrown this place and selling your cures at the flea market."

I wish I had another Ding Dong. I listened to what he had to say. He was right. The retail space for A Dose of Darla had started in the shed until Darla moved it to a booth at the local flea market. She had all sorts of people coming to get her homeopathic cures. And she had been good at it.

I spent most of my teenage years working Darla's booth at the flea market with Oscar right next to me, and hated every moment of it. I always swore I'd never take over Darla's business. As they say, never say never. When Darla died from an apparent heart attack, I did the only thing I could to take care of myself. I took over A Dose of Darla and began to experiment.

Most of the remedies needed to be updated, and since I had always been good in chemistry, I knew I could make them better. Making them better meant doing a lot of combinations of different things and not getting them to explode. Unfortunately, today was not a good mix of ingredients.

"You know I don't want to live in the country with all those scary noises." I knew what Oscar was hinting at.

For weeks, he'd been begging me to get rid of this old house and move to a farm where I could make a real lab, so I could create my remedies the right way. Not in a shed.

"Not in the country." He leaned in a little closer, and said words tentatively as if testing the idea, "I stumbled upon a little village about thirty minutes from here when I went to check out a job opening. I have a good feeling about it. But keep it on the down low."

I drew back to take in his expression. "You can't leave the police department here." I was pretty good at reading him all these years, almost psychic, but the sun cast a shadow on his face, making it hard for me to see if he was serious.

"Shhh." He held his finger up to his lips. "I said down low, not out loud. I will be by tonight to tell you about it. And it really is something you need to consider."

He definitely had my wheels turning as I stood in a puddle of water created by the fire department in their efforts to save the shed, only their efforts had been a waste. Jordan informed me that the fire chief told him the shed was a total loss. As if I needed to be told. All that was left was the cement foundation. Who knew that Thea Sinensis mixed with Camellia was so flammable? I did now. Thank God, because the cure I had been making had been for me. I could really see Mr. McGurtle's face if I had been blow up.

I swear I saw Mr. McGurtle smiling all the way from his front yard.

"Excuse me! Excuse me!" a woman yelled from the other side of the fence. She waved when she caught my eye. "Yes, you!" She pointed at me.

I was glad to see everyone but she had left. The show was finally over and I could get back to work. . . except I couldn't. Not without the shed.

The lady was someone I didn't recognize. The floral A-line skirt was throwing me off a bit, but the black, lace-up booties were definitely awesome. The closer I got, the more she reminded me of a younger version of Meryl Streep, the long blonde hair was long and wavy like Meryl's. Even her nose was small and pointed, only she had hazel eyes and sweeping lashes.

"Are you Darla from A Dose of Darla?" She pointed her laced gloved fingers towards my home.

"I'm Darla's daughter, June Heal." I put my hand out, but she didn't take it, so I pretended to rub them together. "Darla passed away a few years ago. Are you a friend?"

It wouldn't have been unusual for someone out of the blue to show up and visit with Darla. She had friends from all over. Darla was sort of a gypsy type. She believed in free spirit, holistic living, and open imagination. Darla taught me to be kind to everyone and everything.

"No." She scrunched her nose. "Did you take over the business?

"I did." Something in my gut made me wearily suspicious of her.

"You sell something I might be interested in." She lowered her thick dark lashes, and stared at me.

"I, um, sell homeopathic remedies," I muttered uneasily.

Out of the corner of my eye, I could see Mr. McGurtle making his way back across the yard, as fast as his short legs could carry him. Through the herb garden. . .again.

"I was interested in selling them in my store." She pulled a business card out of the top of her glove. "Please come pay me a visit if you are interested. Good day."

I took the card from her fingers and we held a gaze for just a moment. Her eyes wandered over my shoulder. I turned around to find Mr. McGurtle giving her the wonky eye, which was his signature "don't mess with me" look.

When I turned back around, the strange woman was already in her car, pulling away from the curb.

"Do you need something, Mr. McGurtle?" I sighed walking past him toward the house.

Meow, Mr. Prince Charming sat on the top wooden porch step, dragging his tail back and forth. He batted at the cicada darting in the air.

The bottom of his tail was always black from all the wagging he did. It amazed me how, otherwise, he was always pristinely white. I'd assume keeping clean would be difficult for most outdoor cats. But Mr. Prince Charming was not like any other cat I'd ever come across.

"I promised Darla I'd keep a close eye on you," Mr. McGurtle said, stomping after me.

Rolling my eyes, I made it up on the porch before he yelled, "I think you are causing more trouble in your adult life than when you were a kid."

For a moment I stood still, trying to think of an answer while Mr. Prince Charming did figure eights around my ankles, but decided to bite my tongue. It was easier not to argue with Mr. McGurtle.

"Oh, Mr. Prince Charming, must you?" I bent down and flicked the dead cicada into the grass next to the steps with all the other dead ones he had killed. I swear he's on a mission to whack every cicada in Locust Grove. If the cat only knew the town was named after the nasty bugs—he'd be in heaven.

I flung the screen door open, and Mr. Prince Charming ran into the house before me. I closed the door behind me. This was generally how Mr. McGurtle and I ended all of our conversations.

Chapter Two

"You created quite a stir today," said Oscar from the other side of the front porch screen door with a brown sac of our favorite Chinese food restaurant in his hands.

He looked so different without his uniform on. It was hard getting use to seeing Oscar turn from a scrawny, lanky boy into the muscular, hunk he'd become.

Sometimes it was kind of awkward thinking about how it would feel to run my hands through his close cut dark hair, and squeeze a little bit of those muscles. And then I remember how weird it would be since he was really like a brother more than a friend. Still. . .he was easy on the eyes, and single.

I opened the door, and took the bag. I could already taste the egg roll.

"That's how you greet me? Don't you even care how I'm doing or how I feel about my chemistry lab going up in flames?" I stuck my nose in the bag and smelled the yummy goodness.

"I'm sure you'll be just fine, June." He snatched the bag from underneath my nose and took it into the kitchen. "Tell me, were you careless or tired?"

The wooden floors moaned when Mr. Prince Charming jumped off the old radiator that sat just inside the door. He was a sucker for good chicken fried rice. He danced down the hall with his long tail wagging in the air.

"Neither." Inwardly I shuddered at the thought of my carelessness. Though I knew he was right. I hadn't been sleeping well. "I'm just a tad bit tired."

"Are you having nightmares again? Or should I say the dark circles under your eyes tell me you are having nightmares again?" He dropped down on the built-in bench and the cushion made a swoosh sound when all the air flew from its seams.

Mr. Prince Charming took it as his cue to jump up and see what he was going to have for dinner, never mind the full bowl of cat food on the floor.

"It's that apparent?" I leaned and looked into my reflection in the microwave. I tapped underneath my eyes to see if it would help blood flow.

"Is it the same?"

"Yep, the usual." I got a couple of sodas out of the refrigerator, careful for him not to see my face. If I knew Oscar, he was going to study my every move, just like Darla did.

As far back as I could remember I was having the same nightmare of me standing at the edge of a foggy lake looking down into the green murky water and seeing hands wrapped around someone's neck. I always wake up before I can make out whether the person was a man or woman, and it was always the back of the person. The hands are never attached to arms, which really freaked me out.

No matter how much "fairy dust" Darla gave me, the nightmares still came in full force.

"And what are you doing to do about it?" Oscar popped open the can, and then pushed Mr. Prince Charming off the sturdy farm table.

Hiss. Mr. Prince Charming batted air in front Oscar.

"That is what I was trying to do when I blew up the shed." I snickered as I remembered that I had folded the torn up paper with Darla's "Mr. Sandman sprinkles" recipe and stuck it in my pocket right before the explosion. "I might've used a little too much Aconite."

I took the paper out, unfolded it and ran my hands over top it to try to get the creases out. Thank goodness I put it in my jeans, or it would've been ashes by now. I glanced over at the counter where Darla kept an old journal with all her remedies written in it, thinking I should probably either memorize them or make another copy just in case.

30 c of Aconite, 6c Kali phos, 6c Nat suph, 3x passiflora, I continued to count the six ingredients needed on my fingers before Mr. Prince Charming batted at my egg roll while standing on his hind legs.

"No, no," I shooed him away. "Go eat your food."

That was the problem. Since it had always been the two of us, and it was hard to cook for one person, I had always included Mr. Prince Charming.

"How old is he anyway?" Oscar scowled.

"Good question." I thought back to first time I'd ever laid eyes on Mr. Prince Charming.

Actually, it was a long time ago. It was on my tenth birthday. We didn't have a lot of money and Darla had gotten me a birthday cake that read *Happy Retirement Stu.* She didn't even bother scraping Stu's message off. She was good a pretending it wasn't even there, nor the fact that there was a manager's special sticker on it.

All the same, it was a treat because Darla never let me eat any type of sweets growing up. Anyways, Mr. Prince Charming was unlike any other stray cat in our neighborhood, in which there was a lot of stray cats. He had on a faded collar with a tiny turtle charm dangling off it. The turtle had one green emerald stone for an eye and the other one missing. I didn't care. It was beautiful.

Oscar and I asked around if the cat belonged to anyone, no one claimed him, and he just continued to hang around. Darla didn't mind so he stayed. I got him a new collar and kept the charm for myself. Oscar had given me his mom's old bracelet and I hung it from there. I've never taken it off my wrist.

"Well, he's definitely defied the nine lives belief." Oscar couldn't resist Mr. Prince Charming rubbing his tail along his calf. He bent down and ran his hand along the cats back.

"Yes, he has." I smiled remembering all the times Mr. Prince Charming has beat the odds over the past fifteen years and didn't seem to age a bit.

"I see Izzy stopped by." Oscar put Isadora's card back on the table, and then continued to work on his chopstick skills, but wasn't having any luck. "Where's a fork?"

"How do you know her?" I asked as I pointed to the card after I gave him a fork.

"That's what I was going to tell you about," he said as he stuffed his mouth with a big forkful of rice.

"She showed up after the fire debacle." I picked up the card. I still hadn't decided if I was going to see her not. I knew I had to make a business decision whether to grow A Dose of Darla or keep it small. "She wanted to talk to me about putting my remedies in her shop. How do you know her?"

I didn't even know where she was located. The business card said Whispering Falls, but I'd never even heard of the place. I had even tried to Google it early in the day, but nothing came up.

"It was the strangest thing. I was driving and came upon this small town." Oscar's strong jaw line clinched, he grew serious. "Whispering Falls is nothing like I've ever seen. It's its own village of houses, shops, visitors, and is nestled in the woods."

"Where is it?" I asked. He shrugged, but still didn't answer my question. "I tried looking it up and couldn't find it."

If it was really as happening as he thought, maybe it was something I should check out. Going into one store wasn't much work. How many homeopathic remedies could one little village sell?

"It's only twenty or thirty minutes away. Depending on how fast you drive." He smiled, showing off those pearly whites his uncle Jordan had spent so much money on. "And you drive fast."

He was lucky. Darla did good taking me to the dentist every other year. Thanks to Oscar and his uncle, they keep me in floss and toothbrushes. Luckily, I had pretty straight teeth. According to Darla, I had gotten that quality from my dad.

"I don't let grass grow under my feet, that's for sure."

"I pulled into Whispering Falls to check it out. Izzy's place was the first place I walked in. She was asking all sorts of questions about my uniform. She said the council was looking for a cop. We talked a little bit. She asked if I knew anyone who was into home remedies and I told her about you."

Meow, meow. Mr. Prince Charming was begging for attention. I put a little rice in my fingers and let him lick it off.

"So you gave some strange woman my address? I thought you were supposed to protect and serve?" I nervously laughed, half kidding, half not.

Meow, meow. Mr. Prince Charming jumped up on the table and curled his tail around my nose.

"What is wrong with you tonight?" I grabbed him and put him on the floor. He batted at the dangling charm from my wrist. "Stop."

My eyes narrowed, and I studied him for a moment.

"What's up with him?" Oscar tilted his head to the side to get a better look at my disgruntled cat.

"I have no idea. He's been acting strange all afternoon." I ignored Mr. Prince Charming. I wanted to get back to this Izzy person. "How did she find me? Especially my *home*?"

Oscar stood up to throw away his trash. "It's not like Locust Grove is so big. If she stopped and asked about you someone would tell her where you live."

True. It just sucked that she came on the day of the big fire. After seeing all the trouble I've caused the town, she might've changed her mind. No wonder Isadora Solstice high-tailed it after she handed me her business card.

"Did you take the job?" There was no way his uncle Jordan was going to hear of him leaving Locust Grove department.

"Not yet."

"Did you tell Jordan?"

"Nope. No need to just yet."

Now who was being aloof?

"Are you really thinking about it?"

"What if I am?" His blue eyes narrowed speculatively. "I'm a big boy."

Chapter Three

Last night before Oscar left, he gave me directions to Whispering Falls. They didn't seem particularly hard to follow. And since the flea market was only open on the weekends, and my lab had burnt down, and I didn't have anything to do with myself, I jumped in the Green Machine, my two-toned green '88 El Camino and headed toward Whispering Falls.

I'd never been this far out of Locust Grove. The roads twisted and wound around bends, making me drive much slower than I and the Green Machine were used to.

Oscar was right. About thirty minutes of swerves and curves, a clearing popped up as if it had magically appeared.

I pulled over to the side of the road to get a better view of the town. A calmness came over me, something familiar, like I'd been there before.

Nah. I shook the notion out of my head. This didn't look like a place that was forgettable.

"Welcome to Whispering Falls, A Charming Village," read the old beat-up wooden sign. I smiled. It did have a ring to it.

Mewl, mewl. Mr. Prince Charming crawled from underneath the seat and jumped next to me.

"What are you doing here?" I picked him up, looked him square in the eyes, and warned him, "You are going to have to stay in the car."

But I knew better. Many times I'd tried to sneak out of the house over the past fifteen years, but Mr. Prince Charming always either followed me or mysteriously showed up.

The old Green Machine crept down the main street into Whispering Falls. Almost everyone on the sidewalks took time to stop what they were doing and wave at me. I didn't pay much attention to them because the town was nothing like Oscar described it.

It was as though someone came in and carved the town into the side of a mountain. The moss covered cottage shops were nestled deep in the woods, and had the most beautiful entrances I'd ever seen.

Each shop had a colorful awning, displaying its name over the top of the ornamental gated doors. It had a magical feel.

Mr. Prince Charming's paws were planted on the window sill, and he stared out the window as if he knew this was a special place.

I pulled the Green Machine into the parking space in front of Mystic Lights, the shop Isadora Solstice owned. I couldn't wait to see what was inside. The outside was definitely mystic. The hunter green wood door was encased in the most beautiful stone archway. The heavy black metal door handles added to the old world charm.

"You stay here," I told Mr. Prince Charming as if he understood me. I rolled the windows down a little to let some air in, not like I was going to be in there for a long period of time, but just in case.

With my purse strapped across my chest, I grabbed the cardboard box of homeopathic remedies from the bed of the El Camino and walked up the stone steps. I turned around to make sure the cat was okay, and he seemed to have found a nice sunny spot on the dash to curl up and nap.

"Excuse me." A petite round woman used her elbow to push me out of her way, and then opened the door. She looked back at me, gesturing with her stubby fingers. She snarled, "Well, are you coming in or just going to stand there in everyone's way?"

"I. . .yes. Thank you." Tightly I held onto the box as though it was my comfort and followed the woman inside. If my intuition was right, and generally it was, she was not a happy soul.

I decided there was no way she could be a member of the Whispering Falls village. She certainly wasn't friendly. This woman was short and her yellow turban didn't look great perched on top of her short bleach blonde hair. The green and purple cloak perfectly covered what seemed to be a plump-sized woman.

"Izzy, you have company!" The woman ran her eyes up and down, taking in every inch of me. "And she's not from here!"

"I'll be right out," Isadora hollered from the back of the building.

I smiled politely at the woman and sat my box of remedies on the glass counter. With my hands in my pocket, I walked around to see exactly what Isadora's shop sold.

"Are you from another spiritual village?" There was a pensive shimmer in the shadows of her eye.

"A spiritual what?" I laughed. The only spiritual anything I ever got was going to church with Oscar and Uncle Jordan and from Darla's little tidbits of Karma wisdom.

"Um, hmm. I didn't think so," she replied with a heavy sigh and walked into the other room.

We were standing in the middle of some kind of light shop. Above our heads were all sorts of hanging lights with all sorts of crazy shade designs. Some with stained glass, some with globes, but mostly chandelier type. I wondered if most of the houses in Whispering Falls had these types of decorative lights.

I noticed a few snow globes in a glass case, but saw nothing to do with pharmaceuticals or remedies. They weren't like any snow globes I'd seen before. A few were sparkly and the water was black, not clear like most of the snow globes I had seen. There was one snow globe that lit up every time I tilted my head to the side. I leaned in closer, to get a better look.

Ah! I jumped when a face appeared.

"Boo!" The globe radiated purple with yellow lines rotating around like there was static in it and then went black.

I squeezed my eyes shut, and then opened them. It had to be one of those fancy musical snow globes with a Halloween Theme.

"Do you think I like being cooped up in here?" a voice came out of nowhere.

I pinched myself. I had to be in the middle of a nightmare. "Ouch." I shook my arm in the air to shake off the sting. I looked into the globe because it appeared to be dark again.

"Still here." A woman's face appeared. She threw her head back and cackled. Her turban fell off. *Did everyone in Whispering Falls wear a turban?* I rolled up on my toes to see where it went. Her face appeared, taking up the entire globe, making it hard for me to see. "What? What are you looking at?"

"I. . .I," I scratched my head. If this wasn't a nightmare, what was it? I looked around Mystic Lights. The fake blond was nowhere to be found. I looked at the round glass ball and asked, "Who are you? What are you?"

"I'm Madame Torres, voice to the spirits. Who do you seek? Or shall I say who seeks you?" She continued to babble more and more. I continued to stare, not able to wrap my head around what I was hearing.

"This is not happening to me," I repeated over and over, though my intuition told me it was. "This is not happening to me." The more I repeated it, the brighter the globe got.

"Silence!" she screamed, causing her head to spin around and around. "Whom do you seek, June?"

"No one!" I shook my head. Madame Torres was demanding. "I seek no one. How do you know my name?"

"A devils curse seeks to destroy you. Lift us, lift us up to the light and glide June through this stormy life." Her globe illuminated a bright purple and in a flash went to black like when I found it.

"No, no. Don't you wish any evil spirits on me!" I picked up the globe and shook it.

"What are you doing?" The mean woman approached. She stood stiff, her muscles tensed. The blood seemed to have drained from her face. "Did you see something?"

"I. . ." I looked at the snow globe again, but nothing was there. I put it back in its place. Obviously my mind was playing tricks on me.

"Ah, welcome to my little part of the world, June." Isadora walked out of the door she had disappeared into earlier, and held her long skinny hands out. This time they weren't covered in gloves. She had a huge ring on her middle finger that looked like a sleeping cat.

She must've noticed me staring at it.

"Isn't it fabulous?" With her long fingernail, she flicked the cat's back open to reveal a tiny mouse with diamond eyes. "I did notice you had a cat."

"Yes. Mr. Prince Charming." I tried to glance out the door, but couldn't see the Green Machine from here. My eyes wandered back to the snow globe. A light flickered.

Mewl, mewl. Suddenly Mr. Prince Charming was doing figure eights around my ankles.

"You brought him with you." Isadora clasped her hands together, bent down, and picked him up.

"Oh, no you don't want to do that," I warned her. "He doesn't like to be picked up by anyone but me..." *and apparently her*. He was purring so loud, I was sure the woman in the snow globe could hear him.

"I'm so sorry. I left him in the car." I took him from her, and he bounced out of my arms. "Mr. Prince Charming, how did you get out?"

"He's fine. We love cats, don't we, Ann?" Isadora looked over at the other woman. Ann was bent over rubbing her back.

"*You* do," Ann snarled. She made her way behind the counter; she sat down on a stool, and continued to knead her back with her fist.

Isadora turned to me and tried to disguise her annoyance. "Were you looking at my crystal, er, snow globes?" She pointed to the glass case.

"I was. I, ah, have never seen snow globes like that." The one that I had seen the face in was glowing. "They sure do make them fancy now. Sort of like those crazy eight balls."

"Well, they are special. They work off of people's. . .um. . .energy." She chose her words carefully. "Now then, let's go in the back and take a look at your homeopathic cures. Ann, do you think you can do your job and watch the shop?"

Ann's eyes narrowed, and she snipped, "Of course I can."

I took the box off the counter.

Isadora spun on her black, laced up pointy-toed, high-heeled boots and walked to the back of the shop. Mr. Prince Charming and I followed her. Her wavy blonde hair swung side to side along her shoulder blades in step with her long black A-line skirt.

"Don't mind her." Isadora pointed toward the front of the shop, referring to Ann. "She only works here as a favor. She couldn't keep a job in Whispering Falls for the life of her. Now it's my turn to put up with her and her gimpy back."

My brows lifted in amusement. I didn't know Ann or Isadora for that matter and none of it was my business.

"I think Oscar might have misled you about what I really do." I set the cardboard box on her desk and opened it up. I took out the prettiest bottle I had.

Gently I held the lime green glass bottle with the tiny lizard corked on top. The glass had a hint of swirly gold throughout the bottle.

"Stunning," Isadora gasped, taking the bottle. She opened it up and smelled the contents.

"I. . .um. . .don't have cures, just homeopathic remedies that might or might not help what ails you," I stuttered. "No. . .um. . .not cures." Darla's recipes were never potent.

Her long lashes cast a dark shadow on her cheeks. With her eyes still closed, she wrapped her long thin hands around the delicate bottle, and drew in a long, deep breath. She smiled.

"We would love for you to open a shop here." Her eyes popped open and she sat the bottle on the desk. She walked around the desk and sat down. Slowly she opened the drawer and pulled out a packet of papers. "We will need you to fill this application for the council. But don't worry. You are a shoo-in."

Mr. Prince Charming jumped into her lap and dragged his tail along her pointy nose and down her chin. I wasn't sure, but he looked like he was grinning.

"Oh, now I know we have something backwards." Open a shop? Where did that come from? I stood up and put the bottle back in the box. Talking snow globes, a grinning cat, open a shop. . .something definitely wasn't right.

"What? Have I offended you?" She stood up after the cat jumped out of her lap.

"You don't know anything about me. You don't have any idea what I do or even the homeopathic remedies I have and how they help." I wasn't about to agree to anything.

I wasn't a doctor or an expert in the field of homeopathic medicine. I relied on my instinct and Darla's book. That was it. If I opened a real shop and gave someone the wrong dosage, I'd be in hot water. And that was something I tried to stay out of.

As if she read my mind, she said, "Yes, I do know what the berries from a Strychnine tree smells like and what they cure." Slowly she crossed her arms in front of her, and Mr. Prince Charming did figure eights around her ankles.

Traitor.

"Helps with a sour stomach." She grinned, her snow white teeth glistened.

Damn! I bit the inside corner of my lip. She did get it right.

"What does Belladonna cure?" I snapped my finger at her. Belladonna was an ingredient I had never had luck finding.

"Ah." She planted her elbows on the desk and drummed her fingers together. "Are you trying to trick me, June Heal? You're going to have to do a lot better than that." She patted around her eyes with the tips of her fingers. She pulled a container out of her desk drawer. "Belladonna is the main ingredient used in my wrinkle creams."

She handed me the container, which wasn't as nearly as cute as my bottles, and I read the ingredients. *Right again.* "Where did you find this?" I had been looking for Belladonna for years. The women at the flea market would buy that like crazy.

"I will buy it from you when you open the shop." She stood up, and then patted her fingers around her eyes. "It only takes a couple drops on your crow's feet."

"It only takes a little dose," Darla would say when she squeezed the berry between her finger and thumb, letting the bitter liquid drip on my tongue. "Any more than that and it'll kill you."

"June, are you okay?" she asked. She stood over me. "We don't have a doctor in Whispering Falls and could use some of your expertise in the homeopathic field."

She and Mr. Prince Charming walked towards the front of the store and I followed them.

"Listen, I'm not a doctor." I felt like I needed to reinforce my non-doctor speech. "I'm just a girl from

Locust Grove trying to make a living selling stuff at a flea market."

"As you could tell when you drove into Whispering Falls, we are little, well smaller *than* your average village." She twisted her arms and hands in the air, ignoring anything I had to say. "We rely on the earth, nature, the universe to guide us. Let's say we are more on the spiritual side."

For a moment, I felt like I was talking to Darla again. She used to feed me that line of bull when I was a kid. Even though I thought it was bull then, I had really grown A Dose of Darla since I took over. Somehow the remedies I had come up with really did work.

"Can I ask what remedy you were working on when you blew up your shed?" She stood still. But Ann's stool creaked as she leaned a little closer.

"I have issues with nightmares. I'm trying to come up with a cure to help me," I whispered, a little embarrassed to admit I was a grown woman who suffers from nightmares.

"Ah!" Ann gasped, throwing her hand over her mouth. "Torres said nightmares."

Did she say Torres? I looked at the snow globe.

"Ann, can you please go to the back." Isadora's eyes suddenly darkened and she sent Ann away. "She suffers from nightmares, too. You could be such a help to us. Your friend Oscar said you were looking to expand. I guarantee you will not regret moving to Whispering Falls."

She held the papers out for me to take.

"Move?" My eyes clouded over and I grabbed the counter.

"Yes. If you own a shop in Whispering Falls, you have to live here." She flipped a couple pages in the packet and tapped Rule Number Two.

"I'll let you know." I took the packet. I needed to get out of here FAST. "Come on Mr. Prince Charming, let's go home."

"I'll be waiting to hear from you." Isadora chirped as I walked out the green door.

"Excuse us." A couple of grey haired women scurried to the side of the steps to let Mr. Prince Charming and me pass.

"Yes, excuse us." The shorter one giggled and practically hid behind the other one.

"So, sorry." I passed with the intent on reaching my car. . . fast.

"Are you sick? Know someone dying?" I heard one of them call after me.

"Yes, is someone dying?" the other one asked, almost hopeful.

Definitely an odd question to ask someone you didn't know.

"Nope, not that I know of." I brushed my bangs to the side so I could get a good look at them. No turbans. Unfortunately, Mr. Prince Charming must've thought two was better than one. He was doing double figure eights around their ankles. "Mr. Prince Charming, stop!"

He moved faster when I tried to pick him up. He was never this friendly to anyone other than me.

"We like cats," the first one said, bending down and patting the ornery cat.

"Yes, we do." Apparently the second one repeated everything the other said.

I picked him up anyway. I was increasingly becoming confused and the only way out was to get out.

"I'm Constance Karima." She pointed to herself, and then to her twin. "This is my twin Patience."

"Yes, I'm Patience." She giggled. Her green eyes sparkled as much as her teeth.

"Nice to meet you." I noted everyone's fantastic teeth. I ran my tongue along my front tooth that barely overlapped the other. You'd never notice unless I pointed it out.

Mewl. Mr. Prince Charming made his presence known.

"And this is Mr. Prince Charming." I held him tight to my chest in case he decided to jump down. "Have a great day.

Constance stepped in front of me, creating a sudden wind tunnel. Her red housedress swooshed back and forth from the breeze.

"Oh, my." She picked at her short hair nervously. "So, are you sick?"

Mr. Prince Charming kneaded my arms with his back paws.

"Hello, Karima sisters." The green door of Mystic Lights flew open with Isadora standing in the shadow. "Please let our guest leave."

Hiss, hiss. Mr. Prince Charming jumped down, and arched his back. He raced off and jumped in the back of the Green Machine. Like a light switch had gone off, the wind stopped.

The Karima twins tilted their heads and stared at Mr. Prince Charming with a scowl on their faces.

"We were just trying to figure out if he's sick."
Patience's long finger uncurled, exposing a long black
fingernail pointing towards my cat.

Hisssss.

"Yes, sick," Patience repeated.

Isadora's A-line skirt swayed as she gracefully walked
down the steps, coming face to face with me and the
Karima sisters.

"You'll have to forgive my dear friends." She stood
between them, placing a hand on each of their shoulders.
"They own Two Sisters and A Funeral. The only funeral
home in town, and they are always looking for business."

"No, someone's definitely sick." Constance nodded to
Patience who nodded to Izzy.

God, I hope I was nowhere near death, even though my
heart was about to pound out of my chest from shear
freaking out. Whispering Falls was definitely not for me.

"No one is sick," Izzy reassured everyone. Only it sure
didn't make me feel better.

"Wow, nice car," said a voice from behind me.

I spun around to find an older gentleman with black coattails and a top hat checking out the Green Machine.

"I haven't seen one of these since the eighties." He ran his gloved hand down the side of it, and then stopped when he reached Mr. Prince Charming, who was hovering in the bed of the Green Machine. He took his hat off and bowed down. "Good day, sir."

Meow, meow.

I winked at Mr. Prince Charming. I had had enough too. It was time to go home and get back our real life. As a matter of fact, I couldn't wait to get my hands on Oscar Park and give him a piece of my mind.

When I turned back around, everyone was looking at Mr. Prince Charming as if he was the first cat they'd ever seen.

"I guess we better go." I finger waved, trying not to be rude.

"Very nice." The man reached out and touched the turtle charm dangling from my wrist. "Turtles mean protection, and your cat seems to know it."

Slowly I pulled my wrist away from his fingers, causing the charm to slip out of his grasp.

"I guess you could say that." I covered it with my other hand, and brought it close to me. "That's how my cat got his name. He showed up on my tenth birthday with this on his collar and has never left my side."

"Hmmm." He scratched the right side of his mustache, and then pushed the round glasses up on his nose. "I'm Gerald Regiula. I own The Gathering Grove. You should stop in and have a cup. And bring your friend." He glanced over my shoulder looking at Mr. Prince Charming, who had jumped up on the Green Machine's roof and began to clean himself.

"Thank you." There wasn't any more time for me to spare. I had already wasted the few minutes I had been in Whispering Falls, when I should've been in Locust Grove working on Darla's Mr. Sandman's Sprinkle.

"And, if I might add, you should stop in Bellatrix Baubles." He gestured down the road. "She has some amazing charms to add to your collection."

I followed Gerald's eyes because he wasn't talking to me. He was talking to Mr. Prince Charming. And for a second, I could've sworn I saw Mr. Prince Charming nod.

Chapter Four

"Traitor," I scolded Mr. Prince Charming as I drove down the main street. I noticed the dash clock read that I had been in the village for over three hours. I drummed my fingers on the steering wheel. It didn't seem that long. Just like when you went to the circus. You're there for a couple of hours, but you were so entertained that it only felt like fifteen minutes.

Mr. Prince Charming stared at me like he knew exactly what I was saying.

"You were the life of the party." Reaching under the driver's seat, I pulled out a Ding Dong I had stashed in case of an emergency. Hearing an evil spirit was after me definitely qualified as an emergency. The foil crinkled as I unwrapped it, and Mr. Prince Charming knew what was coming next. I tore off a piece of chocolate and fed him. "You weren't the same cat."

Purr, purr. He wiggled his head under my hand and took the chocolaty treat.

We passed a few more of the cottage shops. When someone rushed in front of the Green Machine, I slammed on the brakes.

Mewwwwlll, hissss. Mr. Prince Charming's claws dug in the vinyl dash board where he caught himself.

"Sorry, buddy." Ducking my head around his hanging body to see if I saw anyone on the street. There hadn't been a thud, so I knew I hadn't hit someone, but I swore I'd saw someone.

Creak, creak. A wooden sign hanging from its hinges caught my eye. I gasped, threw the El Camino in park, and jumped out, leaving Mr. Prince Charming in the car.

The sign looked awfully familiar. Scraping the moss off the rotted sign, I gaped in wonder.

"A Dose of Darla."

No. It couldn't be. There was no way Darla had a shop here or any place other than the flea market or I'd have known about it, though it *was* vaguely familiar. Kind of like déjà vu.

I couldn't comprehend what was going on. Dizzy, everything spun around me. I held on to the gate to keep from falling.

The sign hung in front of a small cottage.

Two little windows were covered in moss, and the rest of the outside was covered in the most beautifully wisteria vine. The purple and white flowers grew up and around the front door.

Cautiously, I opened the front gate and moved in for a closer look. Wiping my hands across the window, I took a quick peek inside; only it was too dark to see.

"Can I help you?" Someone's voice startled me, causing me to jump around, landing in my best karate position. "Whoa. I'm only wanting to help." The woman's wonderful low voice was soft and clear. She stood with her hands folded in front of her. She wore a turban like Ann, but she was all smiles instead of snarls.

"Did you see someone out here?" I did a 360 degree turn, keeping my hands in the air, just in case I had to chop someone. I'd seen a man, not a woman with a turban on, run out in front of me. I was sure of it.

"Man? No. If you are looking for a man, you've come to the wrong village." She tapped her temple. "Though I do think there is a romance village with a matchmaker, this is not *that* village." She giggled. "If you are looking for answers you seek while getting those horrid fingernails of yours manicured, you've come to the right place." She gestured toward the little pink cottage, and put her hand out.

I thought she was going to shake it, but she flipped it over, palm up, and drew on her reader glasses that hung around her neck on to the bridge of her nose.

"I'm Chandra Shango. I own the shop next door." A flash of humor crossed her face when she dropped my hand, and then looked at her store. "Cleansing Spirit Spa."

"I sure could use a good massage right now." I could feel my shoulders knotting up from confusion. My nerves were fried. Where had the man gone?

I noticed two large window boxes held a few of the herb plants I had been looking for.

"Drowsy Daisies and Moonflowers." My mouth dropped opened when I saw the flowers perked up, standing at attention. All this time I had been searching the internet to find the ingredients in Darla's recipe book, when I could've traveled twenty minutes south of Locust Grove.

"Darla planted those. It hasn't been the same since Darla's been gone." Chandra had perfectly manicured fingernails. They were painted sky blue with a tiny star in the middle of each one. She looked to be around fifty, with soft hazel eyes and short raspberry hair. "Did you know Darla Heal?"

"Da. . .," I stammered. "Did you say Darla Heal?"

Dizzy again, I was sure I was going to faint.

The tapping of heels caused us to look down the street. Isadora was running as fast as she could in her pointed-heeled boots. Ann was right behind her, her short legs trying to keep up with Isadora, which was virtually impossible.

"You hoo!" Isadora's skirt flew up all over the place, her long blonde hair flowing behind her. Her arms flailed in the air. "Chandra, I see you met June. She's a homeopathic from Locust Grove."

Isadora's chest heaved in and out as she tried to catch her breath. She sat down on the bench beneath the tattered sign.

"You just might need a pedicure after that run." Chandra cackled, clasping her hands together.

Ann finally caught up. Her face contorted like an old cow as she rubbed her lower back.

"Leave it to you to spill the beans." Ann snarled at Chandra. "Izzy had it all planned out and you ruin it."

"That's enough." Isadora stood up and put her hand out for Ann to be quiet. Her eyes were dark and as powerful as her words. "Chandra did no such thing. You are walking a thin line."

Chandra shielded her smile with her hands. There was a state of shock in her expression.

"I told you this was going to blow up." Ann threw her hands in the air. "But no. You had to be all secretive and go behind everyone's back trying to find Darla's daughter when Darla didn't want her to be found."

"I said enough!" Izzy's eyes narrowed.

"And the shed!" Ann stomped. "Do you know how many ingredients I tried before the darn thing would explode?"

I felt the blood drain from my face. Slowly I took a seat on the bench, trying to wrap my head around Ann's words.

My shed? She blew up my shed?

"Look at her. She's definitely nothing like Darla." Ann tapped my foot with her shoe. "Weak, just like her dad. But she did see something in one of the crystal balls."

"Crystal balls?" I asked. I stood up, keeping one hand on the bench to make sure I was stable enough to balance. This bunch was crazy. Crystal balls were for those psychic types. I walked around in a complete circle, carefully looking at each shop and the people milling around. Sure there were some strange shops with some very weird names, and some of the people wore turbans, cloaks, pointy-toed shoes, and other weird getups, but who was I to pass judgment?

"Is Madame Torres in the crystal ball?" I asked.

"Yes," Ann said.

"You've said enough!" Isadora slapped Ann across the face just as a clap of thunder was heard in the bright blue sky.

Ann cowed down. She rubbed her face while she straightened her turban. Her eyes pierced my soul.

"Who blew up my shed?" The question flooded my head and drained out my mouth. My eyes darted back and forth between them. "Are evil spirits really after me?"

"I'm sorry. So sorry." Chandra fumbled with her words, worry evident in her eyes. "I had no clue. I really shouldn't have mentioned your mother."

Flashbacks of the old wooden door came flooding back. Faint memories of what lurked inside the cottage began to emerge from deep in my mind. The richness of Darla's bottles that held her homeopathic remedies glistened inside the shop so long ago. The smell of cinnamon, sage, dill, and thyme entangled and wrapped around me as if I were five years old again. Darla's laughter filled the inside of my head as though she was standing there helping someone with a bad case of gout.

"I've got just the cure for what ails you," she'd say and then grab a couple bottles, combining them into one without even looking at a book or her journal.

Was I expected to move here and take over Darla's old shop? Was this why I had become so good at making remedies? I eased myself onto the bench again.

Stunned, I just sat there while everyone around me yelled. There were so many questions to be answered. But one stuck out in my head. Why did Darla keep this from me?

"Are you beginning to remember, June?" Isadora kneeled down between my legs. "June, dear?"

"I told you she was weak," Ann spoke with a voice full of hatred and her fat finger jabbed at me.

"Shut up!" I jumped to my feet and pushed Isadora out of the way. I shoved Ann so hard, she fell into the wisteria vine and the purple petals fell around her. "And you blew up my shed! You could've killed me!"

"If I wanted to kill you, I would have!" She brushed the fallen flowers off her clothes. "Go home. You don't belong here."

I should go home, but now I questioned where that was. Deep down, I knew I belonged *here*. Even if it was just to find out why Darla had kept Whispering Falls a secret. And what knew about my dad. But I drew back my fist anyway. This woman was going to *get* it. "I'll show you the meaning of hurt!"

The slamming of car doors wasn't going to stop me from opening a can of whoop ass on Ann.

"June?" Jordan and Oscar Park had gone unnoticed when they pulled up behind the Green Machine and stood next to Ann. "Are you okay?"

Turning at the sound of their voices, I took my fist out of the air and put it back down to my side where it belonged.

"I want to press charges!" Ann stomped her foot like a child. "She harassed me. She even threatened me!"

"Of course you do." Chandra stood nose to nose with Ann. "You want to sue anyone and everyone that crosses you. I was a witness, *you* harassed *her* first!"

"That is enough!" Isadora's voice boomed over everyone. Then she said in a softer voice to Jordan and Oscar, "Everything is fine. Go on back to the shop, Ann."

She shooed Ann back down the street toward Mystic Lights, and pointed Chandra back to A Cleansing Spirit Spa, leaving us alone with Oscar and his uncle.

Jaw clenched, Oscar didn't take his eyes off me. He knew something was wrong. There was a magical bond between us. We each knew when the other one was in trouble, and this was one of those times.

I was glad he showed up. He was the only thing in my life that *did* make sense. My entire existence was questionable. I'd even go as far as saying that Mr. Prince Charming was questionable—he was far from a normal cat.

"Izzy, this is my uncle, Jordan Parks." Oscar turned the attention away from me. He was good at doing that when I got myself in hot water, and I'd say that *me* about to punch Ann was dipping my toe in hot water. "I was telling him about the position you offered me."

"I wanted to see for myself." Jordan planted his hand on his holster and looked around. He didn't seem too impressed with the unique village. "I think we should talk about putting Whispering Falls under the protection umbrella of Locust Grove since you are such a small community."

"That wouldn't work." She was on a mission and it showed. "Oscar will have to live in Whispering Falls if he takes the job. He's a big boy, Mr. Park. I think he can decide for himself."

There was an undeniable tension brewing between them. A gate rattled in the distance catching my attention. A top hat peeked out of the Gathering Grove Tea Shop, but quickly slipped back behind the door as it shut.

What had been crystal blue skies had darkened to a dull grey.

Jordan shrugged, and walked back to his cruiser. He called over his shoulder, "Let's go, Oscar."

Oscar looked at Izzy. "I'll take the job."

"What?" Jordan stopped dead in his tracks. "We need to talk about this."

"I'm not ten years old anymore. Izzy is right." Oscar's determination didn't falter. "I can decide for myself. I like it here."

"Wonderful news." Isadora clasped her hands together. The grey clouds parted to make way for the brightest sun I'd ever seen.

Chapter Five

The closer I got to Locust Grove, the more I wanted to turn around and go back to explore Whispering Falls. Granted, nothing went right while I was there, but Madam Torres got my wheels turning with all her "someone's out to get you" talk, and memories that were flooding back. I was on a mission to find out what they knew about Darla and what nasty, mean-spirited Ann knew about my dad. Not to mention, those Karima sisters. I felt my head and I didn't seem feverish, so I couldn't be hallucinating. Plus I remembered! I had been there before, but when? And why did Darla never take me back? Did it have something to do with my dad? Or his death?

As far as I knew, my father and Jordan Park were partners on the police force, and during a traffic stop gone horribly wrong. Jordan and my father had gotten shot. Jordan's crazy looking scar on his abdomen proved it.

Meow, meow. Mr. Prince Charming tapped my hand with his nose. He tried everything he could to get me to pet him while I drove, but I kept my hands on the steering wheel instead. Deep in thought, I tried to figure out the parts of my life I thought I knew.

He finally gave up and batted at the turtle charm.

What did Gerald mean by the turtle charm meaning *"protection?"*

"Have you been protecting me all these years?" Reaching over, I gave him a good scratch under his chin, one of his favorite spots. He didn't answer in his usual cat way.

Not a moment too soon, we pulled into my driveway.

Seeing Oscar's car parked in front of my house was a welcome sight. There were a lot of questions that needed to be answered. I never gave Isadora a definitive answer about me moving to Whispering Falls. According to Oscar, we were.

Since when did *we* become a package deal?

"Didn't you love Whispering Falls?" Oscar had already made it up to the Green Machine before I had gotten out. "Right up your alley."

"No! And that woman burned down my shed." Only ashes remained from my poor burnt down chemical shop.

"What woman?" His eyes bore with questions.

"Ann. She admitted it." That was another reason for me to go back and snoop around Whispering Falls. Why in the world would they want to burn down my shed? Were they desperate to get me there or did they want Darla's remedies so bad they would stop at nothing to get them?

"June, you were in the shed mixing stuff when it blew up." He crossed his arms. "You are saying she hooked it up and blew it up?"

"No." I shook my head. Was it impossible for him to believe me? "The ingredients I was mixing should not have exploded. And she admitted it. I don't know how she did it, but she did." I stomped up to the porch.

Mr. McGurtle cleared his throat from next door.

"Stop eavesdropping!" I yelled across my herb garden. Although I couldn't see him, he was there. He was *always* there. I gestured to Oscar. "Come on."

Mr. Prince Charming jumped out of the car and run up the steps, ignoring the family of possums that had taken residency under them.

"Really?" Oscar shook his head, referring to the cat. "What good is he?"

"Mr. Prince Charming doesn't have killer instincts like most cats." Holding the screen door open with my foot, I unlocked the front door.

Mr. Prince Charming ran ahead of us. I turned on all the lights as we walked down the old hallway into the kitchen. There was still confusion about everything that had happened today. Mostly I was upset because of the way I had talked to Ann. It didn't help matters that the snow globe made me feel crazy. And Ding Dong's made me feel better.

I grabbed a couple of extra ones out of the box, one for Mr. Prince Charming and one for Oscar.

"Thanks." Oscar peeled back the foil wrapper, and shoved the entire chocolaty delight into his mouth. "Mmmm."

He was still the same old Oscar as he was when we were ten years old. He introduced me to Ding Dongs. Oscar's uncle always had the best junk food, where Darla refused to bring the "poison" chemicals into the house, much less our bodies.

I'd sneak out and meet Oscar under the big oak tree on the side of his house, out of view of Darla in case she got up and looked outside, and we'd eat an entire box. Or I guess I should clarify, I'd eat an entire box while Oscar laughed.

"I don't know about moving to Whispering Falls. Even your uncle doesn't think it's a good idea." I bit a small piece off, ran my finger along the cream filling and licked it off. "There is something strange going on in that town."

"I'm a cop. I've checked it out and everything is fine. There hasn't been a crime committed there in years." Oscar helped himself to a glass of milk. "Uncle Jordan is just watching out for us because we are like. . .family. We've got to stick together."

Oscar was right. We didn't really have any family, and I didn't consider Mr. McGurtle family, even though he seemed to put his nose in my business.

"It's just so weird there." It was hard to concentrate on any conversation with the Ding Dong in my hand. I savored every bite. "Granted, I don't make a lot of money at the flea market, but it pays for what I need."

Thank God, Darla had the house paid off. I have no clue how she made ends meet. I always had everything I wanted and she rarely said no, unless it was unhealthy or harmed someone. Plus most of her cures didn't work. Or that's what I found out after she died. That was when I vowed to take over and make her remedies better.

"Who is going to buy my remedies, and how in the world will I ever afford one of those shops?" I shrugged. Did Darla still own the shop? Or did I now own it?

That was definitely something I hadn't thought about.

My thoughts were interrupted by a knock at the door.

Puzzled, Oscar and I looked at each other. No one ever knocks in Locust Grove, especially with the screen door open. Everyone from Locust Grove knew you yell into the house, not knock.

Meow, meow. Mr. Prince Charming greeted the unfamiliar man at the door. His round brimmed hat shaded his face, but I could tell he meant business by his long black overcoat and the briefcase he clutched.

"Hello, can I help you?" I asked the gentleman. Oscar stood behind me. Oscar looked funny in his uniform. Sort of all grown-up. Regardless, I was glad he was there and was wearing it.

"I'm Alexelrod Primrose, a realtor from out of town." He coughed, and flashed his business card. I opened the screen door to take it. "And I have clients moving to the area. This is exactly the house the type of house they are looking for." He curled his nose while looking around. "I wanted to know if you'd be interested in selling."

He held up a sheet of paper with a checklist.

I wanted to ask him if she smelled something funny, but Oscar was too busy asking Mr. Alexelrod Primrose to come in.

Oscar crossed in front of me and held the screen door open. Mr. Primrose walked in. Oscar took him into the family room where Alexelrod made himself comfortable on the couch.

"Last time I checked, this was *my* house." I shoved past him.

"This *is* your answer. Our answer." He moved in front of me, coming nose to chest. A hard chest.

Slowly, my eyes followed up to his crystal baby-blues, only to confirm my childhood best friend had indeed grown into a man; something I hadn't gotten use to or never took the time to notice.

"I don't know," I whispered and bit my lip. There was something exciting about selling it, and moving so I could find the answers to all the unanswered questions about Darla and my dad. I could probably dig around and find out without moving there. My intuition, which had never pointed me in the wrong direction, told me to go for it.

"Think about it. It's what Darla would call fate." Oscar reminded me of the free spirit Darla possessed. When things worked out, she'd call it fate. "She had a store there, and now you've found it."

"Or they found me," I whispered, thinking back to everything Ann had said about Izzy looking for me. Well. . .that's what my intuition told me.

"You know," I paused, and then peeked in at Mr. Primrose, "you're right. I don't have anything to lose. If I don't like it, I will move back. Just not in this house."

"Whispering Falls won't know what happened to them." Oscar laughed and pulled out a packet from the inside pocket of his uniform jacket. *No they won't know what happened to them when I start snooping around.*

"Izzy told me that we have to fill out a membership form and it goes before their city council." He shoved the packet toward me.

I took the papers.

"We have to apply to live in Whispering Falls?" Quickly, I thumbed through the papers and read a couple of the strange questions.

"Izzy said it's just a formality and we will be fine." Oscar nudged me toward the family room. "Don't keep Mr. Primrose waiting."

Before I knew what was happening, I signed on Mr. Primroses' dotted line. Not only did his client's check list include every single characteristic of my house, it included a real check for far more money than my house and Mr. McGurtle's house were worth combined.

"Bye." I waved to Mr. Primrose as he left. I turned to look at Oscar who was still in disbelief with the offer, and I waved the check underneath his nose. "Mr. Primrose is my new best friend."

"He's mine too." Oscar raised his eyebrows when he saw the number on the check. "You don't have to worry about not being able to afford anything for a while."

He was right. I could really try to make a go of A Dose of Darla in Whispering Falls. There was even enough money to make a real lab and order new herbs for different cures.

That was going to have to wait, because first stop on my list was Mystic Lights. I wanted to get a better look at Madame Torres. Maybe buy her with my new found money.

Chapter Six

The next couple days I spent cleaning the house and getting ready for the new chapter in my and Mr. Prince Charming's life. All the crazy things that had happened in Whispering Falls were still fresh in my mind. Several times I resisted jumping into the Green Machine and heading toward Mystic Lights. I didn't want to bring more attention to myself, so I knew I had to wait and fit in before I could show up and start asking questions.

Sadly, my former life fit into three boxes. Darla was never one to keep any type of memories. She said that the best memories were the ones stored in your head and heart, not on paper or photographs. Though I wouldn't have minded a photograph or two of us, a crayon drawing from preschool, or even a report card that showed I was a straight A student. Or something from our time in Whispering Falls. Anything.

Before closing up the last box, which was mostly Darla's, I took out of her collection some incense and held a few of them under my nose. Those were certainly annoying when I was younger, but reminded me of Darla.

My heart ached. I wondered how she would feel about me moving to Whispering Falls. Or why had she never mentioned the town to me? I put the incense back in the box and closed it.

I let out a big sigh, *three little boxes.* I felt for my lucky charm bracelet. That was definitely a memory I'd never forget.

"Oh, no." I looked down when I didn't feel it. Panic filled my gut, instantly making me sick. It was gone. "Oh, no!"

Frantically, I pushed the three boxes along the floor to see if the bracelet had dropped between them while I was packing. Dropping to my knees, I crawled around the house looking for any signs of the bracelet.

I had always planned to buy a real charm bracelet that fit, but Oscar was so proud when he had given it to me, it was hard to make good on getting a real one.

I tore into each box, dumping the contents all over the family room floor, clothing, a few pairs of shoes, some knick-knacks, incense, and cat toys, but no turtle charm or bracelet.

"Are you ready?" Oscar hollered through the screen door.

We had made a pact to leave Locust Grove together.

I didn't answer him. I couldn't. In fact, I opened my mouth, but nothing came out by a god awful cry. If I didn't know better, I thought my heart had stopped.

"I told you to pack your stuff and I'd be by this morning." Oscar shook his head in disbelief. "I can't believe you haven't packed yet, June. What is wrong with you?"

Slumping down on the old couch, I buried my head in the cushion. There was no way I was going to be able to leave without finding my bracelet. There was a knot in my gut. My intuition told me there was something wrong. . .definitely wrong.

"Don't tell me you've changed your mind?" Oscar sat down next to me. He didn't touch me, but for the first time I needed to be comforted. At this point, I'd even let Mr.

McGurtle comfort me. "It's going to be good. You sold this house, furniture and all, and you will really get to work on your remedies."

As if he knew what I needed, Mr. Prince Charming jumped up and dragged his tail under my nose, causing me to giggle from the tickle.

Meow, his rough tongue licked the tear that ran down my cheek. In that moment, I knew everything was going to be okay.

"What's with him?" Oscar asked.

"He's letting me know everything is going to be fine." I dangled my arm in the air. "I lost my bracelet, I'm having nightmares, and Mr. Prince Charming has been getting out of the house at night."

The past couple of nights I've been waking up and finding him on the porch, like he was keeping guard, which was nothing like him. I was sure I had put him in bed with me, but my nightmares were getting more and more graphic.

"Same nightmare?" His deep blue eyes dripped with worry. "Drowning or something?"

"Yeah, something like that." I really tried to see the face of the person who was being strangled under the water, but I'd wake up just as the body would turn.

"I will leave a note for Mr. Primrose to tell the new owners to look out for my bracelet." I put my things back in the boxes, and was ready to leave.

I paused when we made it to the front porch and I glanced over at Mr. McGurtle's place. I hadn't seen him since I told him I was leaving. He made it clear he wasn't happy when he said he had promised Darla he'd watch over me, and my leaving town wasn't in Darla's plan.

"Plans change." I shrugged him off and gave him what few details I had about Whispering Falls. He'd actually heard of it through Darla and seemed a bit taken aback when I told him that Darla had a shop there and I was going to take it over.

Granted, she hadn't been there for years, but I was ready.

Izzy, as Isadora liked to be called, had gotten me in touch with Bellatrix Van Lou, the owner of Bella's Baubles, the only jewelry store in Whispering Falls. She had a small house I could rent until I found something to fit my needs.

On the way into the village, I motioned out of the Green Machine's window for Oscar to go ahead. He was going to start his police duties today, and I was going to give Bella my first month's rent.

Bella's Baubles was like all the other stores in Whispering Falls. A quaint cream cottage with a pink wood door that was adorn with different colored jewels. The sun hit each jewel just right, showing its brilliant color.

I got out of the El Camino. Before I could tell Mr. Prince Charming to stay put, he was already doing figure eights around my ankle.

The store hours were painted on the sign that dangled from the stone casing. *Morning to night.* I was definitely morning.

"Come on," I told him and walked up to the store. The door was incredibly heavy, I had to push with both hands.

Once inside, there was a small entry way that led to two other doors. One of them had a mailbox on it and the other had Bella's sign on it.

Ding, ding. The bell above the door swayed back and forth.

"I'll be right with you." The voice came from the woman who was bent behind the glass counter. I could see her hand working in the case. She laid out pieces of jewelry by color. "I just got some new charms in and I wanted to get them out before the rush."

Charms? Faintly I remember the man in the top hat telling me about this place. I had no clue that my landlord was the owner. I hurried over to see her selection, hoping there was a turtle to replace my lost one. Maybe I could get a real charm bracelet that fit.

"Your signs said the hours are morning to night. I assume you are open." I craned my neck to get a better view of the charms.

She stood up and adjusted her shirt. No turban. Bella's round cheek's balled up through her grin, exposing the small gap between her two front teeth. Her long blonde hair framed her face, and cascaded down her small frame. There was no way she was any taller than five foot two.

"Get back here!" I yelled for Mr. Prince Charming who had jumped on the clean glass counter, and over to Bella's side. I reached over the counter to get him, but he was already out of my grasp. "I'm so sorry."

"You must be June." Her smoky eyes twinkled with laughter. "And I've heard about you, Mr. Prince Charming."

Great! I bet the whole town heard about the new girl fighting with Ann. I chalked one up for the new girl. . .me.

Completely embarrassed, I hid my face when I noticed Mr. Prince Charming had crawled into the jewelry case.

"He must like the lights." There weren't any other explanation. He loved to sun himself. "I'll get him."

Before I got around the counter, he was already out and dropped something out of his mouth on the counter.

"It looks like he wants to give you a charm." Bella waved the silver charm in the air. "A square, Celtic knot. Good choice, Mr. Prince Charming."

Mewl, mewl. He tiptoed around in circles, wagging his long white tail from side to side.

"I'm sorry. We have a strange relationship." I pulled the rent check out of my pocket. I had to get out of there before the darn cat destroyed the place. "Here's your rent. Thank you so much. I will be looking for a place soon."

"Don't worry about it. In fact, the cottage has the most beautiful view. Nothing else in Whispering Falls compares to it." Her fingers worked on a piece of jewelry. "Here you go. Welcome to Whispering Falls."

She uncurled her hand. Between her finger and thumb dangled a real charm bracelet with the Celtic knot attached. She shoved it towards me.

"He wants you to have it. Celtic knots protect you from evil spirits." Her eyes darkened as she moved it closer. "Take it as a welcome gift."

Evil spirits? What was it with this town and evil spirits?

"I. . .I couldn't." I wanted to so bad, and my gut told me to take it. "I can pay for it."

"No." She grabbed my wrist and clasped it on before I could object. "It fits you perfect."

She was right. It wasn't like the other bracelet that I had to clasp on a different link in order for it to fit. I let it fall, showing how well it really did fit.

I told her about how Mr. Prince Charming had showed up on my tenth birthday with the turtle charm attached to his collar and how I had lost it today.

"Fate." She smiled.

"That's something Darla would say." I laughed, but abruptly stopped when we heard a blood curdling scream coming from outside.

We ran out into the street along with everyone else in Whispering Falls to see what the ruckus was about. Constance and Patience were standing by the lake just beyond A Dose of Darla pointing to something. Patience had her face in a handkerchief, sobbing.

"It's Ann!" Patience screamed.

Chandra, Gerald, and Izzy ran to see what she was talking about.

The sky darkened like the lid of an eye.

I reached into my black bag and pulled out my cell phone.

I called Oscar's cell phone. "Something is going on. You better get over to my shop."

Within seconds, Oscar stood next to Izzy, while the rest of us waited in the distance, wondering what they were looking at.

Slowly, Bella and I made our way toward them, as did the rest of the village. There were feet sticking out of the long brush that grew on the banks of the lake. We watched Oscar pull the body out. It was Ann.

Quietly we all waited to see what was going to happen. Oscar was bent over her. Had she passed out? Was she sleeping? She wasn't responding to anything Oscar was doing. He stood up, ran his hands through his dark hair. He turned to the crowd that had gathered behind him, me included.

"She's dead," he announced, but focused on me. "It appears she has been strangled underwater."

There was a collective gasp. I looked around at everyone's faces. Shock and outburst of cries filled the empty air.

"There is a killer among us." Gerald's voice echoed over Whispering Falls and it hung there like a thick fog.

He and Izzy whispered a few words between them before he walked over to me.

"That's terrible." My nerves tingled, thinking about a murder. I couldn't recall any murders in Locust Grove, and I remember Oscar telling me that there was zero crime here.

"We need to talk." He pulled my sleeve toward him. "You need to come to the station."

Constance and Patience ran up. "Do we need to collect the body?"

"Yes, collect the body?" Patience repeated.

"Please." Oscar nodded. He pulled his note pad from the pocket of his uniform jacket and wrote some things down. "I will need an autopsy as well."

The twins didn't hesitate. They folded their hands in front of them, and rushed back to the Two Sisters and A Funeral Home to retrieve the items they needed to get Ann's body.

"They are the coroners too?" I asked Oscar. I shudder to think of Patience's repeating everything Constance said during a coroner's "Y" cut.

In silence, I followed him down to the street. The station was just a little beyond the shop and in walking distance. I glanced back toward the Green Machine where Mr. Prince Charming was cleaning himself on the roof of the El Camino.

The police station was a little more modern than the other buildings. The concrete building had big, round windows that let in a lot of light. No matter where you stood in the office, you could see all the way down Main Street on both sides. I guess this was good for Oscar to be able to keep an eye out.

"Everything is so new." I ran my hand along the gold name plate with Oscar's title engraved on it. The paper sitting on the copier hadn't even been taken out of the packaging. And each pen still had a perfect cap on it. No teeth marks.

"This is serious, June." A sudden chill hung on his words, making me stop and look at him. "There is something you need to know about Ann."

"Well, if you ask me," I said and plopped down on the chair with wheels and slid across the room with my feet in the air, "she probably has pissed a lot of people off with her snide comments. She was rude. Not that I wanted her dead. Think about it, she treated me terrible and I had just met the woman. I wonder how she treated the people she really knew?"

Oscar cleared his throat. "June." His stern voice was cold.

I dragged my feet across the floor to stop the chair. I swung around in his direction.

"Why so serious?" I smiled, hoping he'd lighten up, but I was sorely wrong.

The bracelet that I thought I'd lost dangled in the air from Oscar's fingers.

"Where did you find it?" Excited, I jumped to my feet, and the chair flung behind me, hitting the wall. I grabbed it out of his hands.

"Oh!" Oscar tried to take it back, but I held onto it. "That was in Ann's grasp. I had to pry her fingers apart to get it. Like she had been struggling with someone and she grabbed it off them. Now you have compromised the finger prints."

"What?" I tried to sort through his words. *Ann's hands?* I dropped the bracelet on the floor. I didn't want anything to do with it. "How did Ann get it?"

Having touched something that was in a dead person's hand gave me the heebie-jeebies. *Eww. . .*I rubbed my hands down my shirt.

"I was hoping you'd answer that for me." His voice faded, losing its steely edge. It was a tone I knew well. The way he spoke about his other cases and suspects from Locust Grove was the same.

"Are you accusing me of something?" I drew back and looked him square in the face. "Because if you are, you'd better spit it out, Oscar Park."

"No, but isn't it evident that something is not right. You had words with her yesterday. She accused you of threatening her and then she shows up dead with your bracelet, that you lost, in her cold, dead hand?" Oscar marched back and forth rubbing his chin, and stared out the window.

"Do you honestly think that I killed Ann?" I nervously laughed. If anyone knew me better than I knew myself, it was Oscar. There was no way he could think that I would harm a flea, much less Ann. *Did he?*

"Great." He stood still and leaned to the right to get a better view of the street. "It looks like members of the council are coming this way."

Yep, my intuition told me this wasn't going to be good. I would give anything to have a Ding Dong.

Chapter Seven

Izzy, Chandra, and Gerald hurried down the road. Izzy led the way as fast as her pointy-toed, ankle boots could carry her.

"That's the council?" I asked.

"Mmmhmm." Oscar nodded.

"I wonder what they are saying." I peered over Oscar's shoulder, watching the three of them banter back and forth. It didn't look like a pleasant conversation. Izzy wrung her hands, Gerald gritted his teeth and Chandra had a nervous smile.

Gerald had his top hat off, and held it close to his chest while his other hand twirled one end of his mustache. Chandra tapped her blue nails together.

"You should have seen this coming." Izzy grumbled. She held the door to the police station. Gerald and Chandra kept their heads down as they passed her. She shut the door and locked it. "Ann said that the crystal ball went crazy when June looked at it."

"I don't read the crystal ball. I read palms. Remember?" Chandra's eye blinked rapidly.

The three of them huddled without paying a bit of attention to us.

Palm reading? I had come to grips with the Madame Torres globe, but palm reading?

I reached in my black bag for my phone, trying to remember if I had stored Alexelrod Primrose's number. Surely the new home owners weren't moved in yet. I could probably tell him that I wanted to move back to Locust Grove. Or better yet, move to the country like Oscar originally suggested.

"No." Izzy's head popped up out of the huddle. Her blonde locks swung in Chandra's direction, catching Chandra in the eye.

"Ouch!" Chandra went down holding her hand to her face. "You have got to let me cut that stuff off."

Izzy shooed Chandra and continued to focus on me. "No. You will stay here in Whispering Falls. We have an agreement. Besides, Alexelrod is one of us."

"What?" Oscar looked between the two of us. "June, are you planning on leaving?"

"I. . .I. . ." I held my hands behind me as I backed up to get as far away from Izzy as I could. Truth be told, I was freaking out. How did Izzy know what I was thinking?

Everyone stopped when someone tapped on the door.

"Thank God, Mac is here." Izzy flung the door open to Mr. McGurtle. "Please get in here. We have an issue."

"What's he doing here?" I asked about Mac. Wasn't it enough that I had to put up with this nosy man in Locust Grove?

"Mr. McGurtle?" Oscar stood very still. His eyes narrowed. "What is going on here? I thought I was the law?"

"You are hired by the village council." Izzy circled her long, thin finger between Chandra, Mac, and Gerald. "We are the council."

"I. . .I. . .need a Ding Dong," was the last thing I remember saying before the lights went out.

"June? June, dear?"

I felt a faint wind on my face that I wasn't familiar with, but the rough tongue on my nose I knew. Without even trying to open my eyes, I reached out to pat Mr. Prince Charming. For a moment, I thought I was in my bed at the Locust Grove house until my senses rushed back to me and I realized the smell wasn't different homeopathic ingredients, but the smell of sugary things.

"I think she's with us." Someone patted my hand.

Mewl, mewlllll, Mr. Prince Charming seemed to beg me to open my eyes.

Chandra stood over me, fanning me with her long scarf, her turban sitting cock-eyed on her head. Mr. McGurtle sat next to me and patted my hand.

"Mr. McGurtle, what are you doing here?" I tried to figure out where I was. The round, white table-cloth tables in the room were decorated. Each had a three-tiered cupcake stand and a tea set, as if there was going to be a party. "Where am I?"

"I told Darla I would watch over you." Mr. McGurtle smiled. He took a cup from Gerald. "Drink this."

Chandra put her hands on my back and helped lift me to a sitting position. Once sitting, I could see that we were in Gerald's shop He steeped a few more cups of tea. Izzy stood over him.

"How did I get here?" I was more puzzled than nervous, like I was before. No one wanted to answer me. Oscar was nowhere to be found, which was odd. He'd never have left me in Locust Grove if this happened. "Where's Oscar?"

"Drink, dear." Izzy gestured for Mac to give me the cup. "First, swirl it three times."

Mr. McGurtle got up and let Gerald sit down. Mr. Prince Charming continued to make circle eights around my ankles. As silly as it sounds, it was actually comforting for Mr. McGurtle to be there if Oscar couldn't. Hopefully, Oscar was on the hunt for the real killer.

Pweft, pweft. I spit some of the tea back in the cup. The loose leaves were stuck on the side of the tiny cup.

"Oh, can you flip the cup over on the saucer?" Gerald held a small plate on his hand. Feeling a little leery, I did what I was told. The quicker I did what they asked, the quicker I could get out of here. "Now tap the cup three times."

Tap, tap, tap. The sound of my fingernail hitting the cup echoed throughout the shop.

Gerald took the cup off the saucer and handed it to Chandra who nervously looked at it. He twirled the plate, and intently stared at it.

"Gerald? What do you see?" Izzy stood over Gerald, casting a shadow over me. It was too dark to make out Izzy's eyes.

"What is going on?" I asked, looking into the cup that Gerald held. . .the cup I just drank out of. "What is happening?"

"Give me a minute." Gerald smacked Izzy's hand away. "I see a wavy line in conjunction with an E."

"Oh, that's good." Chandra chuckled bring her hands to her mouth. I've quickly figured out that when Chandra was nervous, she giggled. "An O."

"Shhh!" Izzy warning was quick and fast. "Keep going."

"There is an hourglass without a number. There is a lake with hands." Everyone but me gasped.

"I have nightmares where someone is being strangled by hands, but there is no face and I can't see who is in the dream." I leaned over and looked at the plate. There wasn't anything on it but damp tea leaves. "Um. . .you need to strain your tea better."

Izzy pulled back, exposing the light. Fear, stark and vivid, glittered in her eye. "He reads tea leaves, dear."

"Don't worry. I have a call out to Petunia Shrubwood." Chandra put Izzy and Gerald at ease, but didn't make me feel any better. They ignored me like I wasn't even there.

"Does anyone have a Ding Dong?" If I didn't get a little comfort from somewhere, I was *really* going to kill someone. I could see my purse sitting on a different table. "Get my purse. There is one in there."

Mr. McGurtle scurried to get it and brought it back.

"Who is Petunia Shrubwood?" I didn't even bother savoring my chocolaty treat. I just stuffed it in. I needed instant gratification.

There were so many questions floating around in my head that I couldn't help but spurt them out.

"Petunia will be able to tell us if Ann is back." Chandra giggled.

"Shh!" Izzy took Chandra aside and whispered something that I couldn't understand. Chandra glanced back and me. She smiled.

I'm getting out of here. I stood up.

"Where are you going?" Gerald looked up from the cup, and then at Izzy. "Where is she going?"

"I'm going home." I grabbed my purse. "And by home, I mean Locust Grove."

There was no way I was going to stay another minute in this crazy town. These people were nuts.

Before I could make it to the door, a woman walked in. Her brown hair was pulled up in a messy bun that overflowed. There were flowers stuck in the mess of locks.

"I came as fast as I could." She had a leash dangling from her wrist, but no dog on the other end. "I checked the kennels. I looked around the streets, the lake, but nothing. Not a sign of a new animal."

Mr. Prince Charming sniffed the leash and batted at it. He didn't care that I was upset. *Traitor.*

"That is not what I wanted to hear." Izzy took Petunia into her arms. Petunia let out a little weep, the leash dragging along side of her. "Petunia runs Glorybee Pet Store, along with the SPCA and the grooming business."

I didn't even know there was a pet store around here.

"That means Ann was a bad soul." Chandra's snort was more of a sorrowful sigh. "Bad soul."

"Bad soul?" I looked towards Izzy. She seemed to be the glue that held Whispering Falls together. "Didn't you see her dead body?"

Were these people delusional? Ann was not coming back to life. I knew it and Oscar knew it. *Where the hell was Oscar?*

"If she had had a good soul, I bet she'd been a pig." Chandra drew back and covered her mouth like she had just let the cat out of the bag.

"She might have looked like a pig, but she wasn't cute and sweet like one." Mr. McGurtle joined in on the conversation.

"That's enough." Izzy tried to stop them from saying anymore.

"She not only threatened to sue me, but she called me in front of the council and I'm on the council." Chandra reminded everyone in the room. I took note because it was the first time I heard it. "The nerve of her thinking that the front step of our shop caused her to slip and hurt her back."

"That's right, she sure did." Petunia agreed. "I remember the two of you fighting about that right in front of your shop, and her holding on to her back like she had hurt it."

All of the sudden it was dead silence.

"But I never wanted her dead," Chandra nervously chuckled.

Just for a moment, I looked around the room. Gerald was whispering in Petunia's ear while she tried to cover her smile with her hand. Chandra traced the lines of her hand with her long, blue fingernail, and Mr. Prince Charming continued to do figure eights around my ankles. Oscar was still nowhere to be found.

"What is going on?" I asked. The madness had to stop. I brushed my bangs to the side to make sure I had a good view of everyone.

"Honey, if Ann was a good soul, she'd have come back as an animal." Petunia stared at me with a baffled look on her face. "That's my spiritual guidance. I'm the animal spiritualist."

"What is that?" I was beginning to see what Whispering Falls was all about.

Palm reader, crystal ball, tea leaf reader, and now animal spiritualist? What have I gotten myself into?

She shrugged like I knew what she was talking about, and I wasn't going to stand around any longer. Izzy planted herself in front of the door alongside Mr. McGurtle.

"June, can you please sit down." Mr. McGurtle pulled a chair out at the closest tea table. "I told Darla I would look out for you."

"You've said that over and over, Mr. McGurtle and look where that got me." I crossed my arms. "I'm going to jail for a murder I didn't commit, and you let me move to a crazy town!"

"Honey, we aren't crazy." Petunia shook her head back and forth, a few leaves falling out of the mess. "We are a spiritual village, as in psychics. And apparently you are too."

Everything around me spun around my head, and the room darkened to a dull grey. I gripped the chair to keep myself steady. Petunia's words twisted in my head.

Psychic village. . .everything went black.

Chapter Eight

"Does she do this a lot?" The giggle rang in my ears.

I didn't have to be fully conscience to know Chandra was standing next to me and that I had passed out. . . again. I was sort of hoping all of this had been a nightmare and I was going to wake up in my bedroom in Locust Grove. After all, they had sprung the whole spiritual village thing on me without a warning.

One minute I was flying by the seat of my pants mixing ingredients to sell at the flea market, and the next minute I was number one murder suspect AND a psychic rolled up in one June Heal.

The rough tongue licking my nose reinforced that I was, in fact, in Whispering Falls. And it wasn't a dream.

"I've known her all my life and I've never seen her do this." Oscar's much welcomed voice rung in my ears. It was not a nightmare. "June, can you open your eyes?"

There wasn't a sweet smell to the room. It was more sour. Vitamin like. Slowly, I opened my eyes. Oscar sat on one side and Chandra on the other.

"Hi sleepyhead." Chandra patted my hand. Her turban reminded me that she was a palm reader.

I tried to keep my thoughts free of any negative thoughts or mean-spirited words. Izzy had made it clear that she could read some of my thoughts.

"Welcome home." Oscar smiled as if nothing had happened.

"Are you kidding me?" I whispered. "Firstly, someone is framing me for murder, and secondly, I find out that this is a psychic town. Third, "I held up three fingers, "Mr. McGurtle is involved. And I'm psychic. What's next, you?"

"We need to talk." Izzy came out of a different room with another cup of whatever concoction they gave me at the Gathering Grove.

"No thank you." I pushed the cup aside. "I like my tea without the leaves and tons of sugar."

All the lights in the room came into focus. The little family room had all the comforts of home. The natural wood walls accented the vibrant orange fabric on the chairs and couches. I sat up, taking in my new home. I wanted to go back to my little Cape Cod in Locust Grove.

I shook my head when the last few hours of memories crept back into my head. "Mr. Primrose is a psychic?" I recalled how strange it was that he would just show up at my house with an offer I couldn't refuse. "Why do you want me to live here so badly? Was Darla. . .psychic?"

Psychic or not, I didn't want to be here anymore. Selling remedies at the flea market was looking pretty good right about now.

Fear knotted in my stomach. How could Darla, my mom, be psychic and me not know it? We were poor. We were at our flea market booth every day trying to make ends meet.

"No, she was not. But your dad was." Izzy's words were lagging as she carefully picked them. "He was a spiritualist and your mother was not. But she had a wonderful spirit that was very welcoming to the village. We loved her store."

Oscar didn't seem as taken aback as I was.

"Did you know this?" I asked him.

"Not until today." He looked at Izzy for approval. She nodded for him to continue. He held up a manual of sorts. It was thick. "Izzy felt it was important for me to understand how the spiritual village laws work."

Izzy and Chandra set a cup of tea and plate of cookies in front of me as if I were a child. It was all crazy to me and something I couldn't even begin to understand.

"Your father was our police officer. By Whispering Falls law, there can be only one shop per spiritual family and that includes if you are dating, living, or married to a spiritualist. One shop." Izzy took the packet from Oscar and flipped it open. She pointed to Number Three under the Bi-Laws page. "Your mother opened a little shop and sought some outside spiritual guidance since she wasn't psychic. She made the perfect cures."

Was she talking about *my* Darla? Darla couldn't find half the ingredients her recipes called for and then she'd substitute. Most of her remedies didn't work.

"Outside guidance?" I questioned.

"Someone who doesn't live in the village." She handed the packet back to Oscar. "You don't need to worry about that. Anyway, when your father passed," Izzy looked out the window like she was playing it in her mind like a movie, "Darla, your mother, tried to keep up the shop, but it was hard with a toddler. You."

"You were so cute." Chandra's adjusted her turban. "So cute."

"When you got older, she realized you didn't have any spiritual gifts, and wanted you to have a normal life. That is when she decided to open the booth in the flea market." Izzy ignored Chandra and watched me, intently.

I tried not to show any unusual facial features or freak out. Who was I fooling? They were psychics.

Chandra took my hand and followed the crease along my palm.

She closed her eyes and inhaled deeply. Joy bubbled in her laugh and shone on her face.. "We thought you didn't have any spiritual gifts, but your palm says differently."

I pulled my hand away and tucked it under me.

"You have the gift of homeopathic remedies like your father." The pleasure was apparent in Izzy's smile. "Have you noticed how your remedies really work much better than Darla's? She tried to imitate Otto's, but it was fruitless."

Otto. I hadn't heard my dad's name in years. Darla never talked about him. Now I know why.

"When Otto died, Darla really wanted to make your life whole. Complete." There was a relief in her eyes. She sat down and gently crossed her legs. "She left the village and continued to keep the shop open because we all used and relied on her homeopathic remedies."

"Not that they ever worked." *Tee-hee,* Chandra paced nervously in the round room.

Izzy shot her a look that would make Mr. Prince Charming shudder. Chandra disappeared into another room.

"Mac told us about you making all these new concoctions and how the flea marketing booth was flourishing." She nodded to Mr. McGurtle. "That is when I suspected you might be a spiritualist."

Spiritualist? That didn't' make sense. Just because I have combined some ingredients makes me a spiritualist? My eyes narrowed with speculation.

"As you can see, every shop owner is a spiritualist where their shop name camouflages their gift since we are open to the public," she said.

"What about you?" I questioned Mr. McGurtle. For a spiritualist, he could use some lessons in manners.

"I moved to Locust Grove when Darla took you there." He looked to Chandra who did a little shimmy-shake into the room. "I was watching over the two of you. Orders from the village council."

"Nasty." Chandra chuckled.

"What's with her?" I ran my hands through my hair to make a ponytail using the rubber band around my wrist. I was going to deal with Mr. McGurtle later.

"Locust Grove is nasty. All those wandering spirits crawling around, rubbing their legs together." Chandra did an extra shake with a dramatic finish. "Eeck! Makes me itch thinking about them."

"Spiritualist's that aren't the cleanest of souls or people for that matter, generally come back as the creepier insects." Izzy dusted her hands together.

"Like bees?" Bees scared the living daylights out of me. Once Mr. Prince Charming batted at a bee and the bee turned around and stung me. I told Mr. Prince Charming to never touch a bee again, or if he did, I hoped it stung him.

"Absolutely not!" Petunia drew back, and put her hands on her hip. "Bees are loyal, loving creatures."

She retreated to the back of the room with her head down, nervously fiddling with the flowers in her hair. I guessed I had to be careful about what I said about animals since she was the one who could talk to them.

"We are going to have to explore all of this later. What matters now is that you get situated and figure out how Ann got your charm bracelet." Izzy's A-line skirt and hair cascaded down in unison as she stood up.

"So you know that I didn't kill her since you're psychic and all." I needed them to confirm that they believed me. I rubbed the new charm bracelet and glanced over at Mr. Prince Charming. No wonder he was obsessed with cicadas. Was everything he had done, even picking out the new charm a coincidence, or was he back as someone else?

Nah. He was lying back with his hind leg straight up in the air while he licked himself. No self respecting spiritualist would come back and do that. . .would they? *Nah.*

Izzy snapped her fingers and Oscar handed her the packet. . .again. She flipped it open and pointed to Number Two in the Bi-Laws. "Spiritualists can't read other spiritualists." She handed it back to Oscar.

"Which reminds me." Oscar stood over me with a Ding Dong outstretched for me to take. "I'm going to have to separate friendship from professionalism. Although I don't think you did it, you are the only suspect at this time."

I jumped to my feet and snatched the Ding Dong. "You can't possibly think that I killed Ann. I only knew her for under an hour, and although she was mean, I'd never kill anyone."

Mr. Prince Charming ran over and did figure eights around my ankles. He always knew when I was upset. I've always heard that animals have great instincts when it comes to their owner's emotional ups and downs.

"I'm not accusing you. Besides, village law states that no one is to be arrested for a crime. They just can't move out of the village until the crime is solved. Including murder." This time Oscar opened the packet and pointed out Number Five.

"Are you. . ." My mouth dropped thinking that Oscar could be a spiritualist. "a spiritualist?"

"You need to rest." Izzy pushed Oscar out of the door before he could answer my question. "And you need to get settled into Whispering Falls. You will find all the supplies you need to get started at the shop. Here is the key." She put the old skeleton key on the kitchen counter.

Everyone left, even Mr. McGurtle, who assured me that he would answer any questions I might have dealing with my new life.

I looked around my new home, trying to forget about the murder and my bracelet in Ann's grasp, but it wasn't working. Even Mr. Prince Charming paced along the walls.

How did Ann get my bracelet? Was my nightmare about her? If it was, would these nightmares stop? Why did Darla keep this secret from me? Who was I?

There were many questions I needed answered. And sitting in this house was not the way I was going to get them.

Chapter Nine

My first day in Whispering Falls was turning out to be the worst day in my life. Not only did my lost charm bracelet show up in a dead person's hands, but I'd passed out twice, and found out I was a spiritualist. And I didn't even understand what that was.

Even though it was already dark, surely someone was out and about. I grabbed a Ding Dong off the counter along with the skeleton key to my shop, and Mr. Prince Charming and I headed out on the town.

The fireflies danced around and dotted the night sky creating a little trail down Main Street. No one or nothing was out. It made me wonder if they had locked their doors tight because the new girl had killed one of their own, or just locked their doors out of fear.

Not me. I was on a mission to find out anything I could to clear my name.

Glorybee Pet Shop was the only store with a light on.
Petunia was probably feeding all the animals. I hoped she
was up for company.

The instant smell of animals hit me when I pushed the
heavy electric blue wood door open. It had wavy yellow
metal detailing that resembled the branches of a tree. One
thing was for sure, all the shops in Whispering Falls had the
most beautiful doors that led into amazing stores you'd
never knew existed.

No wonder Whispering Falls was a heavy tourist town.
I'd only wished I could've shared it with Darla or my dad.

Meow, meow. As if he could read my mind, Mr. Prince
Charming stood up on his hind legs and batted at my new
charm bracelet, reminding me that the Celtic knot was
going to keep me safe. At least thinking that was getting me
through this crazy mess.

There wasn't anything normal about Glorybee. I
wasn't sure, but I swear I saw a hedge hog run and then roll
across the grassy floor over to the real life tree that stood in
the corner of the room. As sure as I was standing there, a

bird skimmed the top of my head and landed on a branch next to a grey squirrel.

"You behave yourself." I scolded Mr. Prince Charming before he could get into any trouble. He had been known to chase several birds, squirrels, and chipmunks. I walked over to the tree and as sure as I was standing there, the tree was real all the way down into the grassy floor. It was as if they had built Glorybee and forgotten to lay the foundation.

No wonder I didn't see any animals in Whispering Falls. They all lived here and were living the good life in harmony. Even Mr. Prince Charming sniffed around a few dogs, finally following one to the tree. In a blink of an eye, Mr. Prince Charming was sitting on the same branch as the squirrel, licking his paws.

Please don't swat the squirrel, there was already an accused murderer in the family, we didn't need two.

"I thought I heard someone in here." Petunia peeled the canvas gloves off her hands, exposing the empty leash that was still attached to her wrist, and ripped the Velcro of the beekeeper's veil from her head. "I was collecting the sweet stuff."

She didn't bother batting the handful of bees buzzing around her ear. I cringed at the thought of getting stung by one.

"I was walking by and you had your lights on so I thought I'd stop in and say hi." I wasn't going to jump in and ask about the psychic stuff.

"Welcome to my little part of the spiritual world." She reached up and picked a flower off the tree and stuck it in her bird's nest of a hair-do.

"How do you know Ann hasn't come back?" So much for *not* jumping in. I opened the Ding Dong, tore it in half, and offered it to her. The duck jumped out of the kid swimming pool and waddled over.

"Are you kidding?" She took a bite, inhaled, and closed her eyes. Exactly how they made me feel. She pinched a piece off and gave it to the duck. "This is delicious. But back to Ann. She always made her presence known."

Petunia went about her chores of feeding several of the animals, taking time to talk to each one. They seemed to understand her with their responses of purrs, barks, tweets, and nibbles. A long-haired mutt followed her around. He had a long scarf covering his head and a couple different strands of pearls around his neck. Each longer than the other.

I pointed to him and shrugged. "Does he belong on your leash?"

"Oh no, Elory was a crystal ball spiritualist in a previous life," she whispered with the back of her hand covering her mouth. "He refuses to live without his clothes. You think that's bad, you should've known him when he was alive. He wore at least ten necklaces at once."

I smiled, not sure how to respond to these animals. She talked to them like they were two-footed humans.

"Now go on." Petunia finally shooed the bees away. Quickly, they flew through the store and disappeared through the door she had emerged from. She sat down and used the brush to comb through the Siamese cat's tail.

I wished I had another Ding Dong to give her in case she needed a bribe. I made a mental note to pick up an extra box at the store.

I sat down next to her and picked up the extra brush near her knee. Several dogs ran over to and formed a line. The Great Dane was first in line. Gently, I ran the brush down his back and over his back paws. Petunia brushed a few more before she seemed to remember I was there.

"Poor Ann. No one deserves to die. At least she doesn't have to deal with allergies anymore." She motioned for the next animal in line. The hedgehog. With every brush, it shivered and shook, until it finally curled up and rolled away. "It would be a shame to be allergic to honey."

"She was allergic to honey?" I wondered if Oscar noticed anything funny on the autopsy. Or who does the autopsies around here? "Patience and Constance does the autopsies, right?"

"Um. . .hmmm." She finished brushing the last animal. Mr. Prince Charming. "He is a very sweet cat."

I almost asked her to read his fortune or see if he was someone in another life, but I didn't want to be disappointed. I loved him just the way he was.

"Do you think that Constance would give me the low-down on Ann's autopsy?" I needed more answers. Petunia wasn't being very forthcoming.

"Patience. Ask Patience when Constance isn't around." Petunia's hazel eyes had specs of gold that seemed to glow when she concentrated on something. She stared at me intently. "Patience knows everything going on around here."

Petunia picked a weed next to her leg. She was in her own little world as she crawled around the grassy floor leaving little piles of crab grass along the way. A goat trotted behind her gobbling them up.

Mr. Prince Charming and I left and walked next door to A Dose of Darla. It was time to see what was behind the old wooden door. I had the feeling I was unlocking my past.

When I flipped on the light, my eyes had to be deceiving me. My heart leapt up in my throat, and made my lips turn up into the biggest smile. I hadn't been this giddy since Mr. Prince Charming showed up with my turtle charm.

Carefully, I ran my hands along the tops of the items as I danced to the front of the store. Darla was all about presentation, and I knew she wouldn't disappoint.

The front room where all the hard work of Darla was on display was filled with all sorts of glass bottles of different shapes and sizes.

Lamps were scattered throughout the shop on small tables. Each lamp shade was very ornamental and no two were alike.. I vaguely remember playing with the strands of beads that dangled from some of them when I was a child. They made the shop homey, and it felt like I had come home to a place where I belonged.

There were chalk boards on the wall with the special of the day written in Darla's handwriting. I took my phone out of my bag and took a photo of each board. Darla might not have believed in picture memories, but I did.

Tiered display tables sprinkled the shop floor with all sorts of remedies on them. Although the bottles had dust on them, I knew the remedies inside were good. Luckily, I think there was enough inventory to open tomorrow.

I picked up the feather duster off the counter and shook it in the air. *Cough, cough.* I fanned the air. There was more dust in the duster than in the shop. A quick surface clean was good enough for now.

The back room walls were lined with every ingredient that I had ever dreamed of. Bottle after bottle was in alphabetical order. The dried herbs hung from a clothesline around the room. There were burners, test tubes, melting pots, strainers, muslin clothes, cauldrons and much more. There was a couch, desk, and mini-refrigerator that seemed like a good place to rest if I ever needed to.

There was a cardboard box on the couch. Quickly I rummaged through it. I really wanted to get home and go to bed so that morning would come. I was excited.

The box contained a few odds and ends. A book was wedged in the bottom and I reached for it. I ran my hand along the old leather binding to clear off the dust. Carefully I opened the leather cover. I didn't want it to fall apart.

"Darla's journal," I read aloud. Darla had a journal? "Come on," I gestured for Mr. Prince Charming to follow me. It was time to lock up and go home.

There was enough time to get home, eat a Ding Dong, and read a little bit of this journal before I had to go to bed. Not only was tomorrow a big day, I was hoping that the journal had some answers to the questions I had been seeking.

Clink, clink. I turned the old skeleton key and pushed on the wood door to make sure it was locked. Mr. Prince Charming walked ahead of me with his tail high in the air. It waged back and forth and hit a few fireflies along the way.

Having something of Darla's temporarily made all the bad feelings of the day go away. I'd never known her to have a journal. It sort of surprised me. Darla had no problems expressing how she felt when she felt it. She was always so positive and reminded me that we were no better than anyone or the other way around. She taught me to see the good in everyone.

I was beginning to doubt that with everything that had happened recently. Hopefully, reading some of Darla's journal entries would help restore her belief in me.

My new bed was definitely more comfortable than the one I had in Locust Grove. Mr. Prince Charming curled up in the fold of my arm.

"I open my shop tomorrow," I read Darla's words aloud. *Fun,* I was opening tomorrow too. "I'm a little nervous about some of the measurements being inaccurate. Otto said that it was good, but I still have doubt in my mind. I tell Otto all the time how I wished I had his instincts, his spiritual gift. But if I can't, I hope our sweet little June does."

Darla had doubt? Doubtful was one word I would never use to describe her. She always seemed so confident.

Chapter Ten

"Turn over, turn over," was all I could remember shouting out in my sleep just as I saw the hands slowly peel away from the neck. The head tilted to the side and as if it had one final push, the eyes popped opened, staring at me. They shone with fear.

It was Ann.

My heart nearly leapt out of my chest. It woke me up. Blinking several times, I remembered where I was. Whispering Falls, and smack dab in the middle of a murder. Oh yeah, and how could I almost forget that I'm a spiritualist?

"Mr. Prince Charming?" I called out but he wasn't anywhere to be found. He must've found some sort of escape route out of the house, just like he did in Locust Grove. Darla's journal was lying next to me. I must've fallen asleep reading it. "Eloise," I whispered.

She was going to have to go to the back of my mind until I told Oscar about my nightmare. A little too late, but still it was strange for my nightmares to be changing so much.

I grabbed my cell and dialed him.

"How did you sleep?" There was concern in his voice.

"Good, until the body turned over." I pushed the button on the coffee pot and then looked out the window over the kitchen sink.

It was the most beautiful view of Whispering Falls. The house sat on top the hill giving a great view of all the visitors that were already walking around.

Bella was right. The lush green grass that covered the ground surrounding the shops was vibrant. It looked like carpet.

"What do you mean body?" Oscar asked with caution.

"My nightmare was different. It wasn't the same one." Out the window, in the distance, I could see a little white fur ball galloping toward the house, and it looked like there was something in his mouth. "The hands let go and the body turned over. It was Ann."

"Don't tell me any more until you get an attorney." He pleaded.

"An attorney?" Why in the world. . .*oh, no*. My throat hit the bottom of my stomach. "Are you saying there aren't any other suspects? Only me?"

"I'm just saying that no one else had any issues with Ann that I can find. You and she had a public fight." Oscar was to the point.

"Fine." I wasn't going to argue with him. I knew I didn't do it. Just because everyone around here had all sorts of psychic abilities, I'm sure they were still human and had fights. I did feel a little tension between Chandra and Ann, as well as Izzy and Ann. Hell, Ann had tried to sue Chandra. And what about the statement that Izzy said the first time I went to Mystic Lights about the fact that Ann couldn't hold down a job and it was *her* responsibility. Why was Ann her responsibility?

There was only one way to find out.

Madame Torres.

It was at least worth exploring. I was determined to figure out everyone's relationship and how they were connected to Ann. If I was a betting woman, I'd say Madame Torres could tell me a thing or two.

"June." Oscar stopped me before I hung up. "Don't go around putting your nose where it doesn't belong. You need to let the experts do that. Something will turn up."

He knew me too well. But not well enough to know that I wasn't going to listen to him.

Mewl, mewl. Mr. Prince Charming dropped something near my foot. I hung the phone up and bent down to pick it up.

"You are a thief." The dog charm was cute with the two small diamonds for eyes. "You are making us look really bad. It's not enough that they think I killed Ann and you go off and steal a charm."

What was it with this cat? I shook my head. There was no time to waste. I had to get my hands on that crystal ball, plus it was opening day for A Dose of Darla.

After I got ready, I grabbed a couple Ding Dongs, thinking this could be a stressful day and walked toward Main Street.

I glanced over at Mystic Lights. No thanks to Mr. Prince Charming, Madame Torres was going to have to wait. I had to get this charm back to Belle.

Chapter Eleven

"Good morning." Bella greet us when we walked in. Her store was so crowded. The customers were trying on all sorts of jewelry. "How did you sleep?"

"Um. . .you know, new place and all." I shrugged. Did she really think I slept well? A little thing called *murder* was on my mind. Plus I didn't want to give any details of my nightmare, even though I had to wonder if she could read my mind. I took the dog charm out of my pocket and laid it on the counter. "I'm afraid Mr. Prince Charming stole this from you."

"He didn't steal it. I gave it to him and told him to take it to you." She handed the lady next to me a bracelet with turquoise stones instead of the jade stones.

"I think I like the jade better." The woman pushed the turquoise bracelet back towards Bella.

"No, you will be much happier with turquoise. I promise." Bella's eyes twinkled. She picked up the bracelet and put on the woman.

The woman gasped in delight. She smiled at Bella. "I think you are right."

Bella took the woman's payment, and she left as happy as could be.

"How did you do that?" I asked in amazement. "How did you know she'd like the turquoise one better?"

"It's in her stars." Bella smiled, leaned over and whispered, "I'm the astrologer of the village. You know horoscope and crystal reader."

"Ahh." I nodded. Whispering Falls definitely had a lot of secrets for me to explore. "Back to the charm. You told him to bring it to me?"

"Yes." She picked up a cleaning cloth and cleaned the jade bracelet before replacing back in the jewelry case. "I wanted you to have it. Dog charms help prevent evil spirits from attacking the living. Especially a spiritualist. And I have a feeling someone evil is out to get you."

First off, that didn't make me feel good at all, even though I'd been ignoring my intuition that something evil was lurking. Secondly, Belle's words weren't much different than Madame Torres.

"Out to *get* me?" I felt a little like Patience repeating Constance. "And what do my stars say?"

She was a supposed spiritualist, she should be able to tell me my future or if someone was out to get me.

"Rules of the village, no spiritualist can read for another spiritualist. You must figure your own path." She floated her hands around in the air.

I planted my elbows on the case and put my chin in my hands. "I want my future to be normal like two days ago. That is what I want."

"That might not be in your cards." She smiled before she went on to the next customer. She pointed over my shoulder, out the door. "I think you have a line at the door of your shop."

She was right. A Dose of Darla had customers. Mr. Prince Charming and I hurried out and down the street. There was money to be made.

I slipped into the back door to get familiar with the shop before I opened it up to the crowd outside.

With a deep inhale, I unlocked the door. . .into my new life.

The line of customers was a steady stream. Between answering questions and making up quick remedies, I cleaned all the nook and crannies. Anything and everything that had Darla's handwriting on it, I tucked into a small box that I had found behind the counter.

Nothing seemed to bother Mr. Prince Charming. He found a nice comfy spot on the well worn cushion on a chair behind the counter to sleep on.

It was assuring that I was able to answer questions and mix up all sorts of remedies without consulting Darla's notebook as I had done in years past. It was all coming naturally to me. Maybe I did have a knack for this spiritual stuff.

From the back room, I grabbed of couple of ingredients and threw them in a mixing bowl. I could mix and create while I answered questions.

"Can I help you?" I asked the tall, dark man that had been waiting patiently in the corner of the store as I mixed the remedy to treat hemorrhoids for a waiting customer.

"I'll wait until you are done." He gestured toward my hemorrhoid customer.

I let the ingredients mix, and added an extra spoonful of witch hazel. I picked out the prettiest bottle to put the remedy in. If my customer had to have such an awful sickness, at least she could enjoy the pretty bottle. Unlike the aluminum tubes you get from a doctor.

The hour-glass bottle had the loveliest green flowers glued all over it. But the elegant flower glass cork was the added elegant touch.

"Beautiful," the woman gasped, gingerly taking the bottle from me.

"Follow these directions to a tee, and you will never have an issue again." I assured her giving her a piece of paper that I had scribbled the directions on.

"Thank you," she whispered, touching my hand. "I don't know what it is about this town, but I always leave feeling so good inside."

"Village," I corrected her. "We are a village that cares."

The mysterious gentleman stepped aside to make room for her to leave, and then stepped forward. He glanced around the room before laying a brown package on the counter.

"I'm sorry you waited so long. What is that?" I asked.

He stared at me.

I closed my eyes hoping some type of homeopathic cure would come to me like it had all day long.

Nothing.

I didn't know what happened. I wondered if my spiritual abilities had been zapped.

"What is it?" I looked into his deep, dark eyes for an answer.

Why did I get the gift of knowing homeopathic cures instead of something cool like the ability to read one's mind?

"It's the sweet grass that you asked for." He unrolled the brown wrapping revealing the long stems, some brown, some green. "I didn't come all this way to be shafted. We grow a crop for you every year. And when the winds blow telling us you need sweet grass, I bring it."

"Oh. I'm sorry. I'm new around here. And this whole spiritualist thing is really something I just found out about." I picked up a strand and smelled it. Nothing sweet about it. "And who did you say ordered it?"

"The wind." He crossed his arms in front of him.

The wind? Right. I grinned. So the wind had a soul and he could read it? *Geez.* Now I'd heard it all.

I looked over his shoulders. There was another line forming down the street and he was holding it up.

"I have just what you need." I went to the back and quickly began to mix up bushmaster snake remedy that has a wide range of uses. And not knowing if this guy was crazy, I knew it would help get the chemicals in his mind back to normal.

"June?" Izzy called out from the front. "Do you need some help?"

I walked up to the front and Izzy was talking to the gentleman.

"It'll be just a moment." I put my finger up. "Business is good today."

Izzy leaned back and gestured to the line of customers. "Business is good every day. I see that the sweet grass is here for the smudging ceremony." She patted the tall man on the back.

"Yes." He nodded and put his hand out. "I'm waiting on payment."

"I. . ."I stammered, looking back and forth between them. "I'm a bit confused. Smudging? I thought he was crazy."

Izzy threw her long blonde head back and laughed so loud it made Mr. Prince Charming wake up from his nap.

He stretched and arched his back in the air before he ran out the door.

The tall man also threw his head back, his long black hair falling behind his shoulder, exposing several feathers that were braided into it. Instantly I knew he was Native American and delivering herbs for this smudging thing, whatever that was.

"I'm so sorry." I took a couple hundred dollars out of the register and handed it to him. He was obviously the contact for the village on all things we need from the Native American village.

This was a plus. There were many times I needed something for a remedy in Locust Grove and couldn't get it because no one sold it. If I wanted it, I was going to have to find a Native American to give it to me. Now I had that contact.

He grabbed the money, put it in his pocket and left.

"I'm so sorry. I had no idea," I apologized to Izzy. She took this village very seriously.

"No problem." She looked around. "I'm glad you have put your gifts to work today, and not wasted them at the flea market."

"Izzy?" I stopped her before she left. I looked around the store and made sure no one was around us. "I'd like to buy that snow globe from you."

Her eyes shot through me. "We can talk about that later." Her words were quick and sharp.

"There was one in particular. . ." I was going to tell her about Madame Torres, but she cut me off.

"Have a wonderful day." She turned on her heeled-pointy-toed, laced up black boots, the A-frame skirt twirled, and she walked out.

I was going to get my hands on Madame Torres with or without Izzy's permission, but I had to focus on this smudging ceremony.

I could see the top of Chandra's turban weaving in and out of the crowd.

"I wanted to pop in with a quick hello while I had a person in the mudd bath." She chuckled, and then shivered. "A woman came in for a manicure. Of course I read her palm without her knowing, and talked her into a mud bath. She's going to need a lot more pampering with the stress she's going to have in her life." She tapped her long blue nails on the cash register. "Looks like business has been good."

"I can't complain." Truth be told, I couldn't wait to see how much I had sold today. I was sure I had made more today than I had made last year at the flea market.

I was glad to see Chandra. It gave me an opportunity to ask her a few questions about Ann while the customers picked up the retail bottles and read the homeopathic ingredients that was going to cure them.

"You could tell by my palm that I didn't kill Ann, right?" I was talking about how she had looked at my hand yesterday after I had passed out.

"Oh, dear," she giggled, "it's not my place to judge. According to Petunia, Ann hasn't come back. And we all know what that means."

I assumed she was talking about the whole good soul, bad soul thing. And I didn't even understand all of that.

"You and Ann got along, right?" I leaned over the counter a bit more, pulled my hair behind my shoulder so I could hear her. "Even after she tried to sue you?"

"No one got along with Ann." She tapped her temple. "Gerald did. Once I caught him in here looking through the honey homeopathic cures? Did he ask you about honey cures?"

I wished Chandra would stay on the subject, but she was flighty and always nervous. By her constant laughter, I could tell talking about Ann had made her uncomfortable. Plus she never answered my question about her relationship with Ann.

"I must go. Many customers need their nails done." She smiled. "And a few little life questions answered for them without asking is a nice touch to keep them coming back."

I waved goodbye and helped the next customer.

I wondered if everyone in the village gave their customers little tid-bits about their life using their spiritual gifts. Bella did it with the bracelet and Chandra practiced on her customers. No wonder people came back to Whispering Falls.

I pulled a Ding Dong out from behind the counter and savored every single morsel while recalling what Chandra had said about honey.

Why didn't Gerald get fresh honey from Petunia? Why would he break in A Dose of Darla? A light bulb went off in my head. Did Petunia say that Ann was allergic to honey?

*Hmm. . .*only one way to find out. Patience Karima. I had to get her alone, away from Constance.

After all the customers were gone, I restocked the shelves exactly the way Darla always had, I had one thing and one thing only on my mind. Patience Karima and that autopsy report.

I locked the wooded door behind us, and Mr. Prince Charming and I proceeded to walk down Main Street.

Some of the shops were still open, especially Gollybee Pet Store. I'd imagine her store was the last one closed every day. Who couldn't resist a look at some great animals that cohabit, not to mention the live tree?

I popped my head in to say hello.

Petunia was sitting on the grass floor while the animals and customers milled about. I waved when she looked up. She waved back. There was a bird sitting on her shoulder. A few days ago I would've thought it was strange, it seemed normal. My new normal.

"You hoo."

I looked up and Bella stood on the sidewalk, in front of her shop, waving her hands in the air. "I've got your bracelet."

I had completely forgotten that I had left my bracelet there this morning so she could put the new dog charm on. At this point, I was going to take all the luck I could get. I hurried down to get it from her.

"That was fast." My eyes lit up watching her clasp the charm bracelet on my arm. It reminded me of the little turtle charm, and how much I longed to have it back.

Which reminded me of Ann, and the possibility that she was killed by honey. But why would Gerald want her dead?

"Thank you." I admired the bracelet, and then glanced down the street towards Two Sisters and a Funeral.

The Karima sisters were scurrying down the street.

Gerald came out of the Gathering Grove, and locked the door behind him. He tapped his top hat on his head. He was off to somewhere fast. He didn't even notice us across the street.

"Hello," A whisper grazed my ear.

"Hello," I chirped and turned to see who greeted me. No one but Bella was around me.

"Where is everyone going?" They all seemed to be heading in the same direction.

"It's time for the smudging ceremony. I hope you got the ingredients with you." Bella's brows drew together. She looked confused. "See you there."

There was that word again. *Smudging.*

Chapter Twelve

"Smudging ceremony?" I asked and watched the entire village shut down as if everyone knew what was going on but me. Even Mr. Prince Charming had gotten curious and followed everyone that was walking toward the lake. "I don't even know what that is."

Bella touched her head. "You need to go back to your shop and focus on the smudging ceremony. You will figure out what you need."

This was no time to rely on "you have a spiritual gift speech, use it." I was a fact kind of girl. The girl that used Darla's recipes to come up with her own. I needed a starting point.

"I will let you in on a little secret. A smudging ceremony takes place in the wooded area beyond the lake. There is a large rock that you won't miss. After something, um, say negative happens in the village, we cleanse the village of any evil spirits." We nodded at passerby's heading to the ceremony. "Since you are the new homeopathic spiritualist of the village, you should know everything we need in order to cleanse the village of the evil spirits. I'm just the astrologer."

"But." I was going to protest, but she left without saying goodbye.

I looked back at the Gathering Grove, realizing that Gerald and my questions were going to have to wait. Even the smudging ceremony was going to wait a little bit longer.

I tugged on the big wooden door of Mystic Lights just in case it was unlocked and if it was did that constitute breaking and entering? Of course it wasn't unlocked, so I headed around the back of the cottage shop to check out any other way in.

Each window was locked. I glanced at the cellar doors. My hands gripped the handles, my knuckles white. Without thinking twice about going deep into the eerie basement, I flung the doors open and bolted down the steps.

It was just as icky as I imagined a cellar would be. I pulled the string on the single bulb light. You'd think Izzy would've invested in a nice light since it was a light shop. There were cobwebs everywhere

Phewt, phewt. I blew my way through them and pulled them off my face. I could see the faint green glow from Madame Torres's globe. It led me to the stairs that would lead inside the store.

Creek, creek. One by one the steps made their own melodic song of eeriness. The glow seeped under the crack of the door, getting brighter with each step.

Slowly I put my hand on the knob and tried to turn it, but it was locked. I shook the handle to jiggle it loose.

"Damn," I whispered. It was not going to budge. I leaned my shoulder up against the door and pushed. Still nothing.

"Madame Torres?" I pressed my lips up to the crack. "Can you hear me?"

"What? Where are you?" Madame Torres snarled from the other side. "Isadora Solstice put me in the closet. I don't like the dark." She let out a cry and the glow was gone.

"Madame Torres?" I called for her. "Are you there? I need to know who I need to stay away from. Madame Torres?"

She didn't respond and the crack stayed dark. I had to get my hands on her, but how?

I had no time to try to break in. Evidently I had to perform a smudging ceremony, whatever that was. I made sure that I closed the cellar doors so Izzy wouldn't know I was there. The streets were empty as I made my way to the shop. I couldn't help but peer over my back. If I was in danger like Madame Torres said, and someone was framing me for Ann's murder, surely *they* were watching me. But who?

After I unlocked the wooden door, I stood inside of A Dose of Darla and inhaled—deeply. Surely something was going to come flooding into my spiritualist's body. Nothing but a craving for a Ding Dong came flooding.

I opened my black bag and pulled out a Ding Dong and Darla's journal.

I'd bet Darla had done this smudging thing a time or two. I thumbed through the worn leather journal looking for anything that resembled a ceremony.

"Things you need to know," I read Darla's handwriting out loud. Who was she talking to? Who needs to know what? Was this journal intended for me? As much as I wanted to sit there and read through it, there wasn't time to explore my questions. I dog-eared the page for later reading and continued to thumb through it.

"Intuition?" My gut told me to stop and read it. "Always rely on your intuition. You have always had a great sense of feeling. That is why I think you are a spiritualist like your father. When you really need something, you need to stop and listen to your gut."

I flipped the page. "That's it?" I flipped a couple more pages, but the topics were different. "Tell me something I don't know."

I put the journal in my black bag and strapped it across my chest. I walked to the back room where most of the herbs were hanging and ran my fingers along the bottom-edge of them, trying to "listen to my gut" as Darla had put it. I had no choice but to listen to my intuition.

Sage? Sage was a healer. That sounded good. And that was what I relied on to get me what I needed for the ceremony. After all, it was now my ceremony and I could do what I wanted to.

Which made me think. If I was doing all of it now, who had been doing it? I made a mental note to ask Izzy about it. I wondered if that was a clue to who had been conspiring to make me the village killer.

With all the herbs in my arms, I grabbed the journal, and then I made my way around the lake. I couldn't help but stop where they had found Ann and brush my shoes along the tall grass. I didn't know what I was looking for, but I did hope that Oscar might've missed something. Anything.

The grass parted exposing the muddy floor before the edge of the lake. I bent down when I saw what looked like a shoe print. A couple of shoe prints. And the toes where more dug in than the back of the shoe, as if they stood on their toes for a lengthy period of time. Which someone would if they were holding someone down by their neck, right?

One thing that struck me funny, I was the one who was going to perform the ceremony to heal the village from the killer, and I was the only suspect.

I heard the crowd gathering in the woods. The footprints were going to have to wait. If no one saw them by now, no one was going to be looking anytime soon. Or so I hoped.

Everyone parted when they saw me coming, making a pathway for me to walk to the rock. Bella was right it was a huge rock that had some significant meaning to the village. What the meaning was, I had no clue, reminding me that I had a lot to learn about my new life.

Maybe I should just start reading up about life in jail.

I laid the three herbs I had gathered and put them across the rock. A collective sigh of relief fell over the crowd like I really did something wonderful. That was all I needed. Dramatically, I took apart the sage stalks and light one on fire.

I waved it around me and then danced on the outskirts of the crowd. Letting the smoke of the sage take over the night air. I remember Darla taking her incense and doing something similar. It made me laugh thinking about her and our little dance.

Only now I know our little dances were much more than that. She was trying to keep me safe. But from what, or who?

"Sage is a healing herb. Breathe it. Let it come into your soul. We are in need to heal our village," I repeated, making my way behind the crowd as they swept the smoke close to their bodies.

I made my way back to the rock. I laid the smoldering Sage on the rock to let it continue to simmer and picked up the Cedar stalks.

I lit them.

"If everyone would bow their heads." The cedar began to smoke. I had no idea how to pray, but I'd seen it many times when I went to church with Oscar and his uncle Jordan. It was the only time Darla let me go to church.

"Please drive out all the negative energy and bring good influences into our village."

Everyone had their eyes closed and heads bowed when I went by them, waving the burning cedar over their heads.

I made it to Gerald. He opened his eyes in shock, threw his hands over his mouth, and took off into the dark night.

"Shhhh." I quieted the crowd down. As I continued on my cedar trip around the group, I heard someone make a comment about Gerald and how I must've driven his evil spirit off.

Without hesitation I repeated the ritual of putting the smoldering cedar on the rock next to the sage and picked up the sweet grass, lighting it on fire.

"Everyone!" My voice boomed into the darkness. "Lift up your heads, pray into the smoke. Sweet grass carries your words in the smoke up to the gods."

As if the gods had really spoken, all the four-legged creatures and fireflies gathered into the circle, all their heads to the sky. Remembering they might be good souls that have come back, I made them part of my speech.

"All creatures are welcome." I shook the smoky sweet grass up and down as I walked around. "We are all one!"

I gathered all the clippings in one pile and let them burn together. I rubbed my hands together in the smoke and then brought the smoke to my body, letting it run all over me. I especially brought the smoke up to my head to cleanse any nightmares I might have.

With the smoke billowing above me, I lifted my hands and closed my eyes. "We are entering into the unseen powers of the plants and with the spirits of the ceremony."

Where in the hell did that come from? I opened one eye to see if everyone was watching. They weren't. They were taking it all in.

"As all good relationships, there has to be honor and respect if this relationship is going to work!"

I fell across the rock for a dramatic ending. I waited for a few seconds before I got back up, so everyone had an opportunity to open their eyes and see me.

"Good night." I bowed my head waiting for everyone to leave the circle. "Good night."

With my head bowed toward my feet, I watched Mr. Prince Charming making his figure 8 around my ankles, and purring as if he was letting me know that I did a good job.

"Wee bit of a drama queen?" Oscar clapped his hands together.

"Where were you?" I asked, keeping my voice down because not everyone had left. "I looked for you."

"I was standing by one of the trees in the woods. I didn't want to knock you off your game." He laughed. "Besides, I don't have a spiritual gift and was not invited to the party."

"But I thought you had to in order to live in the village?" That didn't make sense to me. I could've sworn I heard Izzy tell me that. There was so much that had been thrown at me, maybe I had gotten it all mixed up.

"I don't know about that." He pulled a Ding Dong from the pocket of his jacket. "Want company?"

I grabbed it and split it in half.

"I'm always up for your company."

We walked in silence past the lake and up the hill to my rental, savoring every single delicious bite.

Chapter Thirteen

The cleansing must've worked. I didn't have a nightmare and slept like a baby for the first time in years. Even Mr. Prince Charming was curled up next to me when I woke up.

"Glad to see you didn't steal any more charms." I ran my hands down his back and along his tail.

A bit of happiness was in my soul. There were things I had to do, like get a lawyer, figure out how to get a mold of those footprints at the lake, and talk to Gerald.

The sun hit the side-table and illuminated Darla's journal. I was going to try to read a little bit of it before bed last night, but the smudging ceremony mentally exhausted me and before I knew it, my head hit the pillow and I was out. Luckily I didn't have another nightmare, so maybe the smudging thing should happen every night.

I rub my finger over the gold lettering on the old cover. I couldn't help but wonder if she had deliberately left it for me just in case I did find my way back to Whispering Falls and discover that I was like my father—a spiritualist.

Mr. Prince Charming curled up on the pillow, next to my head, when he realized it was going to be one of those mornings. Lazy.

I turned the cover. Mildew and dust tickled my nose. The pages were crisp. Almost fragile as if they were dry-rotted.

Eloise and I made our pact today. The only other person I told was Izzy. There was no way I was going to tell Otto. He's so professional and if he knew I was talking to Eloise, he'd throw a fit. I wish knew what Eloise did to get banned from the village, but Izzy won't tell me and I can't let anyone else know that I found her. She really could be a lot of help around here in making A Dose of Darla a real potion shop. I'm just glad I can help her use her gifts. Plus June loves her.

How in the world did I love someone I didn't even remember? If I loved her so much, why wasn't she in my life? I was sure that Izzy could answer those questions.

Mewl, mewl. Mr. Prince Charming had enough of Darla's journal.

"Fine. Let's get going." I threw the bedspread back and planted my feet in the shag carpet. It was way better than the old hardwood floors the Cape Cod had. Quickly I glanced at the next entry before I put the journal back on the table. There didn't seem to be anything that popped out at me. Nothing that couldn't wait until later.

We made our way to our new kitchen. No different than every other morning, I made my coffee and threw a scoop of cat food in Mr. Prince Charming's bowl. I had no idea why I bother. He ends up eating my leftovers or I just make double.

Out of the corner of my eye, I saw someone walking down the empty street of Whispering Falls. It was still early and the streets wouldn't be filled for a couple of more hours.

I could see a woman with short red hair and wore a long cloak. She was mumbling something and swinging a long chain.

"What in the world?" I squinted to confirm that she was swinging smoke out of a ball at the other end of the chain.

Izzy came into the light wearing a different A-line skirt, a purple choice today, and the same pointy-toed ankle boots. She gestured towards my house. I ducked in case they saw me spying on them.

"Who are you and why are you looking up here?" This was a feeling I didn't like. After all I was still the only suspect in Ann's death.

It's wasn't me they should be looking at. I can't say my smudging ceremony technique was a gift or more of bull on my part, but I did know that Gerald got sick and left. According to smudging "rules," if someone gets sick during the ceremony, they have evil souls.

I took a sip of my coffee and looked at Mr. Prince Charming. "I can drink tea in the morning instead of this." I set the mug down and went back into my bedroom to get ready.

I had plenty of time to grab a cup of tea before work and ask Gerald a few questions, plus find out who that woman was.

By the time we had gotten out of the house, the streets were already beginning to fill up with visitors, and lines had formed in front of many of the shops.

Of course there was a line at the Gathering Grove. It seemed to be the big hangout for everyone in the village. Plus it was the only place in Whispering Falls to eat.

"Hi, June." Chandra's hands were filled with a sac full of goodies. "I love to have these sitting out when clients come in. It's all about pampering the soul, and it helps to pamper the stomach. I'm surprised to see you here."

"I thought I'd try out what I hear is the best cup of tea in town." I held the door for her.

"And see if Gerald is an evil soul?" She chuckled.

"No, why would I think he was evil?" He did run off during the smudging ceremony which may have meant a couple of things. One, that he was a bad soul, or two, that he was hiding something. I picked number two and that was exactly why I was there.

Before she could answer, a flurry of visitors pushed their way through the door.

"Stop by and I'll give you a free manicure." Chandra held her sack tight. "We can catch up then."

"Ok!" I shouted over the crowd.

I got mixed up in the group and continued to make my way to the register to order my drink. There wasn't going to be any time to question Gerald because the long line in front of me was going to take up any free time I would have before I needed to open the shop.

I looked around, but couldn't see over everyone's head. Gerald was nowhere to be found, nor his top hat. Mr. Primrose, the realtor, was standing a couple of people in front of me in the line.

"Mr. Primrose, how do the new owners like my old house?" I was curious to see how they were getting along.

"Um. . .June dear, that was bought by the village. We need you here, so you can visit anytime you'd like." His face turned red. "I'm not good at lying. I'm sure it would be fine with the council if I told you the truth."

If they didn't sell my house, then maybe there were some clues to what happened to my bracelet. I had the bracelet on when I went to bed on my last night there. I didn't have it on when I was packing the boxes.

"Hello, June!" Bella shouted from behind the counter once I got to the front of the line. "That bracelet was meant for you."

I lifted my hand up and admired it with her. It was a perfect fit, but I still missed my turtle. Though I wasn't sure if I wanted it back because it had been in the clutches of a dead hand.

"What are you doing here?" I asked. There had to be a reasonable explanation. "Where's Gerald?"

She looked around before she answered. She leaned over the counter and whispered, "He's ill. But hopefully will be back tomorrow. Quick frankly, I'm surprised to see you here."

That was now the second person to tell me that in less than ten minutes.

"Everyone seems to be surprised to see me." I was beginning to believe there was a rumor going around about me that I should be in jail.

"You tried to kill me!" Gerald screamed from across the room. He rushed over. His bottom lip quivered. Or what was once the outline of his lips. His eyes were swollen so much that all I could see were little slits. With his fists clinched to his side, he growled, "You do not belong in this village. You are nothing like Otto or Darla!"

I tried to kill you? My eyes bulged. I was unable to think, and nothing was coming out of my mouth. Everyone stopped drinking their tea, and eating their goodies. All eyes were on me.

"I. . ." I gasped for air.

"I. . .I what? Didn't think you'd get caught? Well, I've got a call into that police officer from Locust Grove, checking into your background!" He shook his fist at me. "You will not be able to practice your spirituality here until you are found not guilty! Order of the council!"

A collective gasp filled the air. My legs felt like they were filled with lead, unable to move.

"Don't do that to her, Gerald." Bella moved from behind the counter and took me into her arms. "She didn't know that you are severely allergic to cedar."

Cedar? I quickly recalled my specifically getting into the cedar portion of last night's smudging ceremony. I especially fanned the smoke near the members of the council to show them that I might know what I was talking about with the spiritual stuff. But truth be told, I was winging it the entire time. Why in the world did I listen to my gut like Darla said in her journal?

"If she's a spiritualist, she'd know." His jaw clinched and he glared. "Get out! I will let you know when the committee is going to meet."

I ran out without looking back. I slammed into someone, knocking them down.

"June?" Izzy was laid out flat with her purple skirt flung in the air. She fought the skirt tooth and nail to keep the crinoline down, but it was winning.

"I'm so sorry," I gasped reaching for her hand to help her up. Instead I fell on the pavement next to her and burst into tears. "I'm a failure. I'm not a spiritualist. I should've never moved here."

"That is nonsense." She stood up and brushed herself off. "Get up and come with me."

I did exactly what she told me to do. By the time we made it down to Mystic Lights, a crowd had gathered outside the Gathering Grove and everyone was staring at me.

I briefly told Izzy what had happened in the Gathering Grove, including how I picked the herbs out for last night's smudging ceremony.

"First off, you didn't try to kill anyone. We rushed you into moving here." She unlocked the gate to Mystic Lights and once inside she locked it behind us. "Secondly, that is what a spiritualist does. You are listening to your instincts, the higher powers are telling you what to pick. And it worked! I had Eloise confirm it this morning."

"Eloise?"

"Yes, she is a spiritualist who uses the power of incense to cleanse or empower the client. She's amazing."

Izzy talked in a rush. "She said that everything is going to fine in the village. Just a hiccup or two. Maybe Gerald is one of those hiccups. But as a spiritualist, you know you can't read another spiritualist unless they let you." She tapped the crystal ball sitting on the counter. It wasn't Madame Torres. I wished it were.

The face appeared from the dark liquid and didn't take her long-lashed eyes off me.

Was the person in the crystal ball wanting to read me? I'd never believed in any of that stuff, like Darla—until now. I glanced around Mystic Lights to see if I could find Madame Torres, but the glass globe wasn't anywhere to be found.

Focus, focus. I peeled my eyes off of the shadowy face from the other crystal ball.

"Can you tell me a little more about Eloise? And how to find her?" I asked. The face in the crystal ball continued to watch me and every move I mad.

"She only visits every once in a while. There's no need to worry about Eloise. I'm sure you'll meet her one day." She tapped the crystal ball with her long fingernail.

"It's just that Darla had some kind of agreement with her." I shrugged, and lied. "I only want to find more out about my past."

That really wasn't a lie. I wanted Eloise's help. If Darla trusted her, maybe I could trust her in helping me clear my name.

"Really," Izzy's voice boomed, "there is no need to contact Eloise. I don't recall her ever knowing your mother."

Liar! I wanted to shout and point, but she wasn't going to budge. One way or another, I was going to find Eloise.

"What about the crystal ball I want? Where is it?" I looked around again.

"That old thing? It's probably been put away. I can't remember. You need a new one. Once you settle in and we get this whole murder thing behind us, I'll give you a lesson." Izzy walked over to the gate.

I wasn't interested in a lesson. I was interested in what evil spirit was out to get me. Right now, Gerald seemed to be the only evil spiritualist out to get me. Or was he the one framing me? There was no way I was going to ask the relationship between Gerald and Ann. Izzy made it very clear she wasn't interested in helping me.

"Anyway, why don't you take the day off and let me talk to Gerald when he calms down."

She patted my shoulder and nudged me toward the door. "I will let you know what happens. Just take some time for yourself today."

A customer hurried through the door.

Sure you will. I was beginning to realize I couldn't believe a word that came out of Izzy's mouth. I was going to have to solve this thing on my own if I wanted to be clear. She was right about taking time off. Not only was I going to take the day off, I was going to drive back to Locust Grove, see if there are any funny footprints around my old house.

I turned back around to face Izzy when I remembered what Gerald had said about me not being able to open my shop until I was found not guilty.

"What about my shop?" Lines formed between my brows.

"Oh, that." She grabbed the crystal ball off the counter and shooed me off so she could help the next customer.

I took it as a cue to wait on her to talk to Gerald. I couldn't leave the shop closed for long. It was my income. It was how Mr. Prince Charming and I ate.

"Are you going on a trip soon?" Izzy asked the customer as she rolled the cloudy, round glass in her hand.

"Yes." The customer drew back. "How did you know?"

"Let's just say I see sailboats in your future." Her eyes lit up when a smile curled on her face. "Be sure to get some Dramamine from your doctor. You are going to have a fabulous time."

The customer nodded and they continued to carry on a conversation. I was sure Izzy was going to be dishing out even more advice.

Chapter Fourteen

I pulled up to the old Cape Cod, and my heart sank for Darla. Even when Darla died, I had always felt a presence. I didn't feel that in Whispering Falls. Maybe it was the memoires that made me nostalgic. I could only hope the journal would help fill that void.

The Green Machine seemed to groan with happiness when I turned it off. Mr. McGurtle's house was as lonely as mine. I wondered if he ever came home or just stayed in Whispering Falls since I wasn't his responsibility anymore.

I grabbed my black bag and strapped it across my chest. I walked around what was left of the shed before I went in the house. Just a few boot prints from the firefighters and ashes were all that was left. Not even a piece of the test tubes I used to mix my crazy concoctions could not be found.

I pulled on the screen door and it was unlocked just like it always was. Instantly a familiar smell consumed my soul. . .home.

The old floor creaked as though I'd never left, and the furniture was still in place.

I wiped a tear that had fallen down my cheek. *Home sweet home,* I sighed. Only I couldn't come home until I cleared my name in Whispering Falls.

With my shoulders back, I inhaled. I came here to do a job, and to find any evidence that someone had taken my bracelet.

I went back outside and looked around, especially underneath the windows. The only way someone could break in, at night, would be to climb through one. That was exactly how Oscar use to get in.

Many times I'd wake up and he'd be standing there without me ever hearing him come in. Darla finally caught on when she had some of her herbal pots in every window of the house, and the one in my room had been trampled.

She never planted grass under my window because of Oscar. It became a joke that Oscar never came in the house through the front door.

I bent down and looked at the dirt. There was a little earth scuffed up, and I took a better look. It sure looked like the shoe print in the mud at the lake where they found Ann.

I took my phone out of my black bag and flipped through the photos to find the one that I had taken of the lake shoe print.

"Hot damn!" I clicked the phone to camera and took a couple shots of the print.

I ran back into the house and down to the basement. Once Darla wanted to be creative and make a cement mold with color broken glass. She said it was all the rage. Apparently not in our flea market. She never sold one. But I knew there was still cement mix in the basement.

I mixed up a small batch and before I headed out the door, I remembered I had left a stash of Ding Dongs under the last basement step in case there was ever an emergency. I stuck my hand under the old wooden basement step and felt around until I had the round delicious treat in my finger tips.

Heaven. I held it in one hand and the mixture in the other. I trotted up the steps to the first floor and out the door to get the evidence I needed.

I poured the wet, grainy liquid on the shoe print. The package said that it would take an hour to set. Since it was so old, I figured it would take two.

I was mentally exhausted and nothing sounded better than my Ding dong and a good nap in my bed. I flicked my shoes off, put my bag next to the bed and got out my Ding dong. Comfort set in as I curled up and savored every single chocolaty morsel. Before I knew it, I fell asleep.

Turn over, turn over… I begged the victim to show me their face. The hands continued to squeeze around the victim's neck.

"Turn over!" I sat straight up in my bed. I brushed my bangs to the side. Sweat had plastered them to my forehead.

My heart was pounding and my hands were shaking. My cell phone was ringing. I dug in my bag to get it. It was Oscar and I sent him to voicemail.

I didn't feel like re-hashing what happened in the Gathering Grove or tell him that I had another nightmare.

"June?" I heard a voice call out from the front porch screen door. "June?"

With my purse in hand, I slipped my shoes on and went to the front door. Jordan Parks was standing there in full uniform.

"Hi." I opened the door and stepped out on the porch. "I was going to come see you."

"You were?" There was tension in his face. "I was going to come to Whispering Falls to see you."

Gerald's words rang in my ear, *"I already called Officer Jordan Parks to find out about you."*

"I heard. Whispering Falls hasn't been a good move for me." I walked down the steps, jumped over the cicada cemetery, and checked on my cement mold.

"What's that?" Jordan asked.

"I'm going to find out who is framing me for murder. I think they broke in my house and stole my bracelet off my wrist when I was sleeping." I touched the mold and it was dry.

"You? Sleeping?" Jordan laughed. He did know everything about me. After my dad was killed, he did everything he could to help me and Darla out. One time I thought he was going to marry Darla, making Oscar and I brother and sister. Yuck!

"I know it sounds far-fetched, but I think this is the print." I picked up the cement block and looked at the perfect mold.

"You need to let Oscar do his job, and that's what I told Gerald." We walked back to the front of the house. "But I still want to talk to you. Maybe I can help out. I thought they sold your place?"

"Not yet." I wasn't going into the whole spiritual routine. I was already accused of killing someone, attempted murder on another. I didn't want to add crazy to the list.

"I'll stop by one night." I did need his advice, but I wanted to wait to see what Izzy found out. "How about you make me some of that famous box spaghetti?"

"You got it, kid." He waved. I watched him leave, and then ran into the house to grab the bag of cement. I was going to make more mix and get the print from the lake.

The entire way back, I couldn't get my nightmare out of my head. It was the first time I had a nightmare while napping. Up until now, they had always taken place at night.

It was the same as every other time. There was a head underwater with hands around the neck. Only the head was different this time. The hair was darker and longer. Not like Ann's. But the hands were still the same.

Before I knew it, I was back driving back down the main street of Whispering Falls. I parked the El Camino in the empty space in front of A Dose of Darla. I took the cement bag out of the bed of the Green Machine.

"Where have you been?" Chandra giggled, twisting her hands together. She stood underneath her little pink awning of A Cleansing Spirit Spa. "I heard what happened with Gerald after I left the Gathering Grove this morning. What's that?"

I rested my hand over the word "cement" on the bag and tucked it close to my chest. "It's an ingredient I need to make a cure."

"Oh." She slid a little closer and leaned in to get a better look at what I had.

"I'll be by later." I peeled a note off the gate, and unlocked it. Once inside, I locked it behind me.

"June," I read the note out loud, "please come by Petunia's and get me. I need you to make me something. ~ Mac McGurtle."

I hardly finished the note when there was a knock at the door.

On the other side stood Mr. McGurtle and Mr. Prince Charming.

*Hmmm. . .*when we lived next door to each other, they despised one another.

"I saw Mr. Prince Charming hanging around the gate, so I knew you had to be around. Besides, your old beater sticks out like a sore thumb." He gestured to the Green Machine.

"Hey, that's a classic." I always had a special place in my heart for my ride. I held the note up in the air, and opened the door wider so he could come in. "I was just reading your note."

He followed me into the shop. I noticed the items that needed to be restocked, but why bother when I wasn't able to sale anything because Gerald thought I tried to kill him. Plus I was possibly going to jail for killing Ann.

I motioned for him to follow me to the back of the store where the ingredients were stored. Luckily, there was a small refrigerator stocked with pop and a couch to relax. Before all this mess, I loved the idea that I could come to work and get through the day or go hang out in the back mixing all sorts of potions and relaxing. That was a far-fetched dream.

"I was wondering if you could make me a lucky mojo bag?" He drummed his foot on the floor and staring at me.

What in the hell was a mojo bag? Much less a lucky one? If I knew, I would have made *me* one, because luck didn't seem to be on my side at the moment.

"What's in a lucky mojo bag?" I rubbed my neck. This was obviously one of those things only a true spiritualist should automatically know. And I was a little leery on the whole instinct thing. I saw where that got me. "This is awful!"

I fell on the couch, face down and sobbed. There had never been another time when I wanted Darla so bad. Not even Oscar would do.

Mr. McGurtle sat down next to me. "This is the exact thing that Darla thought was going to happen."

"Tell me. Tell me everything." I rolled over, sat up and brushed my tears. Darla had confided in him. Maybe he could help me.

"There isn't much to tell." He stood up and paced. His eyes darted nervously around the room. "I'm a spiritualist. I read tarot cards. And I knew your dad and Darla from a long time ago."

He paused and looked at me.

"Kiddo," he pointed between the two of us, "you and I use to play together in this shop. We got along great. So when Darla wanted you to have a 'normal' childhood, we knew we couldn't just send you out in the world with a spiritual gift."

"Why not?" I had seen plenty of celebrities endorsing the psychic hotlines on TV.

"A true spiritualist has to be embraced and live around other spiritualists. Especially when they are children. So I agreed to move to Locust Grove and live next door when the council asked me to. Darla was happy, until she got sick. That is when she made me promise to watch over you. But you were grown and doing great, so I keep my distance." He cleared his throat. *Grown?* I was barely out of high school. "I know you have the gift, but you have put up a wall. You can't accept the fact that you are a spiritualist and that is causing the blockage. You have to learn to accept who you are. Darla wasn't sure if you had it or not."

"What makes you so sure I am a spiritualist?" I crossed my arms in front of me.

"Do you remember when I had the indigestion issue and I asked you for a remedy?" He asked.

I nodded. I remember looking at Darla's recipe and knew that something was off, so I added my own touch, albeit oyster shell clippings crushed and mixed in, and it worked.

"You whipped up that mixture without even thinking about it." His eyes glittered with inner light. "It worked like a charm. All of your remedies began to help a lot of people in the village. I didn't tell the council, but they found out. That is why I was shocked to see Izzy standing in your yard. They never contacted me to let me know they were coming for you."

"Coming for me?" I drew back.

"They would never make you come, but they have a great way of persuading you." He laughed. "And this whole thing with Ann is a mess. They aren't even looking into Gerald. Everyone wants to overlook that."

"Overlook what?" I was never one for gossip, but if this was going to help me, then I was all ears.

"Ann has been after Gerald for years. From what I heard, he gave in a few times then and she wouldn't leave him alone. But with the council taking away her spiritual shop and banning her from using her gifts, he had to be careful. Him being on the council and all. I even heard they met at the Gathering Grove the night before she died. But that's just what Petunia had said." He threw his hands up to his mouth, but it was too late.

"The council banned Ann?" What I needed to know was who really didn't see eye-to-eye with Ann. And if they had reasons to kill her. "What in the world did she do to get banned?"

"I've said too much. Just forget everything I said." He wrung his hands together.

I heard every word he said, and put Petunia on my list of people to question, along with Izzy. And I could ask Izzy about Ann getting her 'gift' taken away. Ann must've done something really bad.

"Who told Petunia?" I asked.

"Did I say Petunia?" His brows drew. "I'm not sure who said it. Anyways, a lucky mojo bag is a bag that is filled with items that will keep me safe. I think a lot of the village might be requesting a few since there is a killer on the loose."

I went over to the work station and picked up two pieces of red cloth from the cloth bin and quickly hand-stitched the seams. I'd never sewn a button on a shirt, but something took over me and I whipped it up in no time. Mr. McGurtle and Mr. Prince Charming watched in silence.

I grabbed different blue items for peace and serenity to put in the bag. The items would surround him, giving him peace of mind. Even though I've never used a bat's wing for anything or even thought of it, for some reason I had a feeling to use it. I walked up and down the rows of shelves that started at the floor and didn't stop until the ceiling. They were stocked piled with all sorts of ingredients that weren't available to me in Locust Grove.

"A pinch of bat wing, a few touches of root, a couple coins, and a couple of carved amulets." I repeated everything I was putting in the bag. I scribbled Mac McGurtle on a piece of paper and stuck it in the bag. I pinned it shut and handed it to him. "Thank you, Mr. McGurtle. You have helped me more than you know."

I wanted to tell him to watch over his shoulder because everything I put in the mojo bag was all intuition and lately my intuition had been off. . .way off.

When he left, I locked the door behind him. I had the urge to make more mojo bags and sell them in the shop. Not just protection bags, but all sorts of bags like happy, money, good luck, and peace bags.

I worked way up into the night as Mr. Prince Charming worked alongside me. He would bat at different ingredients and I'd stick them in. It was like he knew what he was doing, but I thought I knew better than that.

As I created, my mind was free and let me think about why anyone would want to frame me for Ann's murder. I understood why Gerald would have it in the back of his head that I had tried to hurt him and I was sure he was going to come to his senses. Or at least hoped Izzy had talked him into his senses.

I was definitely going to make a visit to Petunia's tomorrow and pick her brain about Ann and Gerald's relationship. And find out from the two sisters if there was honey in Ann's system. I wondered how many people knew about Gerald's distaste for her, not that I thought he killed her—well maybe.

Chapter Fifteen

When I finally decided it was time to go home, I quickly mixed up a small batch of cement. There was no way someone would see me in the middle of the night, go to the lake and pour the mixture in the shoe print.

Outside of A Dose of Darla, Mr. Prince Charming stood as still as a statue looking toward Gollybee Pets. A long thin shadow ran across the street and darted off toward Mystic Lights.

"Hey!" I yelled, wondering who it was. Chills ran up my legs and traveled down my arms.

The shadow stopped, briefly turned and looked at me. The glowing teeth were the only thing exposed in the upward grin. Then it was gone.

The shadow made me feel the same way I had felt when I thought I had hit someone with the Green Machine the first time I had come to Whispering Falls.

"Let's get out of here." I played with my charm bracelet. Bella said Mr. Prince Charming had picked out protective charms. There was no better time like the present to be proteted.

Mewwwl. Mr. Prince Charming let out one long, low groan. We watched a shadow move closer to us, but from the opposite direction.

The gait was fast, but the night wind had whipped up and was quicker. A top hat flew into the middle of the street. Gerald ran to get it, but not before he looked around to see if anyone saw him.

Mr. Prince Charming and I slipped back into the shadow in the entrance of A Dose of Darla, so Gerald wouldn't see us. It made me wonder if he was breaking into Gollybee like Petunia had said he'd broken into A Dose of Darla.

I reached in my black bag and grabbed my phone. With a few clicks, I took the pictures I needed for that 'just in case' moment.

Once Gerald was out of sight, Mr. Prince Charming and I made our way to the lake.

The starry sky lit up the dark night just like a flashlight, reflecting off the lake. I bent down at the edge where I had seen the print and parted the grass.

Mewl, mewl, hiss, hiss.

"I know. It's creepy out here." I looked around to see what Mr. Prince Charming was in an uproar about, but chalked it off when I didn't see anyone, just a few fireflies. And he batted at those, sending them off flying in a straight line.

I poured the mix into the shoe print. Luckily the print had hardened making it a perfect mold.

"I don't think we've met, this time?" A voice broke the night silence, almost making me tip over into the lake.

In the shadow of the moon, she stood between us. Her scarlet hair cut close to her head, and long flowing cape gave her a sophisticated look that I hadn't seen anyone, other than Izzy, look like in the entire village, making me think that she was part of the council.

"I'm Eloise Sandlewood." Her emerald eyes light up like the fireflies that flew around her. "It's nice to see you again, June."

"Eloise." Relief settled in my heart. She had a lot of answers to my questions about my past and Darla's. "Have we met?"

There was a part of me where I wanted her to embrace me and tell me all about Darla and their past. But the other part of me wanted to run.

"Long ago." Her lips curled into a smile. "You wouldn't remember me. I'm an incense spiritualist. I help cleanse things, plus I have a few other odds and ends up my sleeve."

"I saw you in the middle of the street with Izzy this morning." I gestured. "In front of the Gathering Grove."

"Yes, I was cleansing the shop to help Gerald recover faster." Her brows lowered. "I know you didn't know he was allergic to cedar. He has even more problems than that."

My ears perked up. "What do you mean?"

"I don't know. It's in the smoke." She pulled a small metal ball out of her pocket, along with a match. She opened the ball where there were some herbs rolled up, flicked the match with her fingernail, and caught it on fire. Touching the match to the ball, the herbs smoked until their flowery scent reached into the air. She swung the ball back and forth by grasping the long chain. "Nice to see you, June. If you need anything, you will find my house in the woods behind the gathering rock."

"I do need something." I tucked a piece of hair behind my ear. "I need to know how you helped my mom."

Eloise's shadowy figure turned around. The brightness of the moon cradled her face like a spotlight. Her eyes glowed brighter as she spoke. "Your mother was my best friend. Do you have a few minutes to visit me either tomorrow or the next day?"

"What's wrong with now?" Why wait?

"It's a bit complicated and I really don't want anyone seeing us here." Her cloak swooshed when she parted her arms and gestured toward the lake. "I live beyond the woods, behind the rock. You will rely on your instincts to find me."

"What *is it* with following instincts?" I rolled my eyes. "That is all the advice I could find in Darla's journal that she had for me. *Follow your instincts, June.*"

Eloise's eyes drew dark. "She left a journal?"

"Yes. That is how I knew about you and your little agreement."

She looked into the darkness. "We must not talk about it here. If you want to talk, you must use your instincts to find me." She disappeared into the black night.

There were no footsteps, nothing. She was gone. Yes, I would go see her. I had to find out the big secret behind the arrangement.

I didn't bother taking a look at the cement mold. I knew it needed more time to dry. I had nothing but time. First thing in the morning, I was going to make a visit to see Petunia. I'd pick up the mold then.

Mr. Prince Charming trotted ahead of me. With every snap of a branch or swish of the grass, I jumped. That was one thing about Whispering Falls. You didn't know who was watching you at any time.

Eloise had my mind reeling, making it hard for me to sleep. I grabbed Darla's journal off the table and pulled the covers up to my neck. Mr. Prince Charming nestled underneath the cover in the crook of my arm.

"Eloise made the funniest potion today. Talk serum. We gave some to Izzy and she wouldn't shut up. I had to make her leave before Otto got home or I was afraid she was going to spill the beans about Eloise. I didn't want him mad, especially now since the council approved A Dose Of Darla."

That was the last thing I remember reading before I fell asleep.

Turn around, turn around! The hands floated away, and the head bobbled side to side. *Just a little more to the right.*

My body shook and I woke up in a dead sweat to a banging on the door.

Groggy, I pulled back the sheet from my damp body, and noticed the clock read nine o'clock AM. I hadn't slept that late since I was a teenager.

I jumped out of bed to see who was at my house. Mr. Prince Charming stretched his front legs out in front of him, yawned, and then followed me to the door.

"I hear you are making new friends right and left." Oscar held up a bag of muffins from the Gathering Grove.

I rolled my eyes, moved out of the way, and let him in.

Meow, meow. Mr. Prince Charming made his presence known.

"Not for you." Oscar put the bag up in the air a little more, so Mr. Prince Charming couldn't bat at the bag. But that didn't help. He was up on the counter before Oscar sat the bag down.

"Gerald called Uncle Jordan, accusing you of killing Ann and trying to kill him."

"He's crazy." I shook my head. "How was I to know he was allergic to cedar of all things? Not like he knew Ann was allergic to honey."

"What do you mean?"

"I mean you need to get that autopsy to prove my innocence. When will the Karima sisters have it complete?" Not only were Constance and Patience the owners of the funeral home, they were the village coroners. "According to Petunia, Ann was highly allergic to honey. And Chandra caught Gerald breaking into A Dose of Darla stealing honey supplements. Why would he steal honey when he could get real honey from Petunia?"

I paced back and forth trying to figure out why he'd steal it, when it hit me.

"Supplements don't show in the blood stream!" I pounded my fists in the air. I knew Gerald was up to something. "As a matter of fact, I also heard that Gerald and Ann had something going on. But Ann got on Gerald's nerves and he dumped her. She was chasing him around and he was annoyed with her."

"That doesn't make him a murderer."

"No, but he did have tea with her the night before she died. And maybe he gave her the honey supplement." My head was beginning to hurt.

"Who told you all that?" Oscar questioned.

"People." I shrugged.

"I've been working on this case for a couple of days and no one wants to talk to me."

"They don't' trust you. That's why Gerald called Jordan." I didn't know if that was true, but it sounded pretty good. "Now, about that autopsy?"

"I should get it back any time now." His brows met in the middle. "No you don't, June Heal. I know that look on your face. You let me handle this investigation before you get yourself into any more hot water." He threatened me and I don't take threats lightly.

Oscar was crazier than half of this town if he thought I was just going to sit back and let him try to exonerate me. I was on a roll and Petunia was next in line.

"Did you hear me?"

I did, and remembered that someone else was going to die, but who?

"June, are you okay? All the blood drained from your face." Oscar knew me too well.

I worked around my new kitchen making a fresh pot of coffee to go with the muffins.

"Spill it." He took me by the shoulders. "Even Uncle Jordan said that you were acting funny yesterday. He said he stopped by the Cape Cod when he saw the Green Machine there."

"I needed some comfort and you were too busy. That's why I went to the Cape Cod." I didn't want to tell him, but I knew I couldn't keep quiet. "I'm having nightmares again. It's a different person. The hair is different, but the killer's hands are the same."

Nervously, I bit my nails. A nasty habit I had broken years ago, but my nerves had gotten the best of me. I had to make an appointment with Chandra to get them painted. I wouldn't bite them if they were painted pretty.

Oscar ran his hands through his hair, sat down in one of the kitchen chairs, and propped himself up on his elbows. "Do you think this is your 'gift'? Can you see when someone is about to die?"

That was one 'gift' I did not want. But when I thought about it, most of my nightmares, when I was a child, did come true in one fashion or another. Once I lost a shoe and had a nightmare about Darla being mad, then another one where I had lost it. I went to the place I saw in my dreams and it was there.

Another time I had a nightmare that I fell off my bike and got stitches, only the next day it happened to Oscar. Darla always said that I had an active imagination.

"Oscar?" I gasped, thinking he might be right. "One problem is that I don't know the outcome until I dream it, and then it is too late. Or at least it was for Ann."

"Is there anything else in the nightmare that you can remember besides the head? Can you look around and see if there are any clues on the hands? Markings?" Oscar asked some great questions, but how was I going to manipulate my dream?

I pushed the muffins aside. I'd suddenly lost my appetite.

"So now what?" I waited to hear my fate. Were they or weren't they going to charge me with murder?

"We will wait until Gerald gets better and the council can meet to discuss all the evidence." His appetite wasn't affected. He stuffed a half of a muffin in his mouth.

"I did find a journal from Darla in the shop." I hesitate for a moment, wondering if Oscar might want it for evidence, but I continued. "There really isn't anything in there but how she moved us to Locust Grove."

"Really? Anything else about the village?"

"I haven't gotten that far. If there is, I'll let you know. But nothing earth-shattering." Even though there weren't any mind-blowing events in the journal, it was still nice to have her journal. Which seemed odd, because Darla never kept anything.

After Oscar left, I went over the clues with Mr. Prince Charming.

"Chandra and Ann didn't get along because Ann took Chandra before the council to sue her for her back problems."

Meow.

I paced between the kitchen and the family room.

"Gerald broke into A Dose of Darla to get a honey supplement. Ann was in love with him and drove him crazy. He had tea with her the night she died. Alone. Only, in Whispering Falls, we are never alone."

Meow.

"And Ann was banned from practicing her spiritual gift." I wondered what her gift was. "Plus she lost her shop." I threw my hand in the air. "Oh! Don't forget about Gerald slipping into Gollybee last night."

The questions about Ann getting banned were for Izzy to answer.

Now there were three visits on my list. It shouldn't be hard to make a quick visit to each of them since I couldn't open A Dose of Darla until I hear from the council. I had some time on my hands, and I was going to use it to prove my innocence.

Funny, the council consisted of two of the three people I needed to talk to.

Mr. Prince Charming couldn't care less. All he wanted to do was bathe himself.

"Fine. I'm going to get my mold, and then stop by Gollybee Pets to pay Petunia a visit."

As soon as he heard Gollybee, he ran over and did figure eights around my ankles before we headed out.

Chapter Sixteen

I was careful not to be seen when I picked up the mold at the lake on my way to Gollybee. At a glance, the cement mold resembled the shoeprint that I had cast under my bedroom window in Locust Grove. I hid it under my shirt and dropped it off at the shop on my way to the pet store.

Mr. Prince Charming didn't wait around for me. I was sure he was already there.

"What took you so long?" Petunia was pruning back the limbs on the indoor tree.

"How did you know I was coming by?" I handed her a mojo bag that I grabbed from the shop.

"Him." She pointed to a very high branch, where Mr. Prince Charming was sitting next to a chipmunk. "Oh, I love mojo bags. Thanks."

"You're welcome." I didn't have a really good way to beat around the bush. I had limited time before Oscar heard from the council or even looked for more clues. "So tell me about Ann and Gerald having a fling."

Petunia's expression completely left her face.

"I heard that they were having a fling." I acted as though I couldn't tell that she was surprised that I knew. I reached up and picked a few of the dead leaves off some of the branches, petting a few animals as I went.

"I don't know anything about that." There was a slow burn in her voice. "Why would I care about such silly things?"

"Oh, I thought you had something going with Gerald." I shrugged it off. I knew I had gotten her goat. Her face was fire engine red, matching the rose buds she had decided to stick in her bird's nest of hair.

"Why in the world would you think that?" She huffed.

I looked around the branch to see her face. "I remember when I was at the police station and he was whispering in your ear. You didn't seem to mind it."

She swallowed hard, held her chin up and pulled her mouth up in a sour grin. "That is ridiculous. Don't go around here spreading rumors, June Heal."

"Are you sure?" I gave her another chance to come clean. "Because he was sneaking in your shop last night or at least that's what I have on my phone."

I pulled my phone out of my bag and flipped through the pictures to find Gerald grabbing his hat and then going into Gollybee.

"What do you want from me, June?" Petunia leaned up against the tree and crossed her arms. "We can't tell anyone because you aren't supposed to date other shop owners. You can date people within the village, but you can only own one shop. Ann found out and she threatened to tell and we couldn't have that."

"So you killed Ann?" I gasped

"No!" A voice boomed from the back of the store, and then followed by heavy footsteps. "No we didn't kill Ann."

Gerald peered out of nowhere. If I'd known he was there, I wouldn't have questioned her. This was a time I probably should've left it up to Oscar.

"It seems awfully funny that Ann found out about the two of you and the next thing you know she's dead." I started to walk backwards in case I was next. "And she was allergic to honey. Not to mention that you broke into A Dose of Darla to steal honey supplements. I even heard that you met with her for tea the night before she died. Did you lace it with honey?"

"Don't be ridiculous!" His voice rang out. Not only did I squirm, the squirrels ran for cover. "I wouldn't hurt Ann." He walked towards me with Petunia closely behind him.

I shook my finger at him. "What about A Dose of Darla?"

"It was before you came to town and wreaked havoc." He did fist pumps in the air. His top hat teetered and tottered. "No one had used those remedies in years. Ann was having some weight issues and honey helps with weight loss."

Like I didn't know that. "I'm a homeopath spiritualist." I reminded him. "Remember?"

"She wasn't allergic to the supplement. And she couldn't find anyone to give it to her since she was semi-banned from the village." Gerald stood with his hands on his hips.

Banned, semi-banned, which was it? Either way banned wasn't a good thing.

Mr. Prince Charming jumped out of the tree, and stood between me, Petunia, and Gerald.

"We didn't kill her. You have to believe us, June." Petunia pleaded, taking Gerald by the hand. "Ann has a lot of enemies here. Not just us."

"Yes, but the number one reason for murder is jealousy. And if Ann wanted Gerald. . ."

"No, Ann wanted us to lose our shops like she did. Gerald took the supplements to keep her quiet. She'd demand things and we'd get them for her. But we'd had enough. And we told her that." Gerald twirled his mustache. "We are planning on telling the council tonight after they discuss your situation."

"My situation? You mean the fact that you accused me of trying to kill you and being the number one suspect in Ann's death. That situation?"

"I know you didn't kill Ann." Petunia pulled a rose out of her hair and offered it to me. "Besides whoever killed Ann doesn't live around here."

Okay, she had me for a second.

"How do you know that?" I wondered if she was still accusing me since I wasn't from there.

"The teenagers told me." She was confident, and Gerald nodded.

"Teenagers?" First off, I hadn't seen any teenagers, and secondly, who believed teenagers?

"The fireflies. They are a group of teenagers. Duh!" She wiggled her hands in the air. "They stay up all night and sleep all day. They tell me everything. Even about the little meeting between you and Eloise last night." She let out a deep, gratifying sigh.

Fireflies? Obviously she knew that Eloise wasn't supposed to be anywhere near the village. I wonder why Ann could live in the village but not Eloise. Did Petunia know Eloise and Darla were friends?

"They said that they didn't recognize the figure. Couldn't tell if it was a man or woman, but they were positive it was someone they hadn't seen before." A smirk crossed her face. She gestured between her and Gerald. "So you will let us talk to the council before you tell anyone about us?"

I wasn't about to take their plea deal, but held off. This was not a peace offering.

"It's crucial that you tell them tonight or I will tell Oscar everything I know." I turned to go out the door, but turned back around. "Tomorrow! I will tell him tomorrow!"

I stomped out of Gollybee with Mr. Prince Charming on my heels, and headed towards A Cleansing Spirit Spa.

Everything that they had said played over in my head. They were being blackmailed by Ann and that seemed like a really good motive to kill her. I was still going to check out the allergy.

I didn't know who to believe in Whispering Falls. Everyone seemed to have something against Ann, while all I did was have a verbal disagreement with her. And everyone talked in circles, they knew something about everything.

The grey walls of A Cleansing Spirit Spa instantly made you feel relaxed when you stepped in. Never mind the trickling waterfall features Chandra had sprinkled throughout the spa that echoed the life of 'Zen resides here', but the lit candles added to the ambiance of the silence.

The low tantric music streamed throughout the spa. I couldn't tell if the Buddha's that were strategically placed were staring at me, or mocking me with the laughter on their faces.

As I walked by one, I made sure to rub the belly. Darla did that every time she would pass one of the many booths at the flea market that sold the plastic statues.

"June! "Chandra giggled. "I'm so glad to see you."

I wiggled my poor chewed up nails in front of me. "I'm in desperate need of a manicure or I won't have any nails left."

"Come on in." She gestured for me to take a seat at the table next to her. "Go ahead and take your shoes off and stick your feet in the soapy tub."

Since I couldn't open the shop, I had plenty of time on my hands.

Chandra adjusted the light over the customer's hands she was working on. She filed away. Everyone once in a while I noticed her turn the client's hand over and let out a little "*hmmm*".

I sat down and slipped off my shoes. The water was nice and warm. I didn't come in for a pedicure, but it looked too inviting to pass it up. My toes played with the rocks in the basin.

"Do you remember the last time I came in to get a manicure?" The customer asked, her eyes darted between Chandra's eyes.

Chandra nodded.

"Well, I played the lottery like you told me to and I won." The woman whispered. A huge grin was on her face. "I couldn't believe it."

"Did you sign a prenuptial agreement before you got married?" Chandra didn't acknowledge the woman's comment about the lottery.

The woman drew her hands back, leaving Chandra's hands empty. Slowly she shook her head.

"You need to see a lawyer, honey." Chandra patted her client. The client slowly got up and collected her things before she walked out the door.

"Poor girl." Chandra clucked. "She's in for a nasty divorce."

"You could've let her down easy." I suggested.

Chandra rolled her chair over to the basin and put a towel on her leg. She patted her knee for me to put my foot up on it. She dried it off and worked away.

"Sometimes readings don't go the way people want them to go." She took out a file and used it on my heel. I flinched from the pain. "How long has it been since you had a pedicure?"

"Years." The last one was at the flea market from another booth owner, and then it was nothing like this. It was in a metal tub with bubble bath. "Do you always read your clients?"

"That's why they keep coming back." She winked and finished up the other foot.

I followed her over to the manicure table.

"You sit here and I'll get the manicure system." Chandra hurried off behind a cream colored partition.

There were two manicure tables, two pedicure chairs, two massage tables, two of everything, but only one of Chandra. The muffins, from the Gathering Grove, were neatly placed and untouched next to a display of cups, orange juice, and a pot of coffee.

"Do you get a lot of customers?" I questioned, because the place didn't looked touched.

"I do" She reappeared and had a silver tray full of all sorts of tools and different colors of nail polish. "Especially after they had a friend like the last one that came in and I tell them some lucky numbers. I don't know what those numbers mean. The spirit tells me to tell the client the numbers. I do what the spirit says."

She took my hand rubbed some oils on it, focusing more on my palms. When I tried to flip them over, she'd flip them back and run her long blue fingernails down my creases.

She rubbed the oil in my cuticles and pushed them back with a pointy thing on the end of a plastic stick. Her turban wobbled back and forth with her every movement. "Never had a manicure?"

"No, how can you tell?" I tried to see what she saw.

"Your cuticles are a mess. And you are keeping a secret." Her eyes glowed with excitement.

"I thought the rule was that we aren't supposed to read other spiritualist unless we give them permission."

"Ah, rules." She cackled. "So many rules. Don't you know that spas are where women gossip? So dish."

She looked up at me, but was still busy pushing back my bad cuticles.

"Nothing. I'm just trying to figure out who killed Ann so I can clear my name."

"I think you are hiding something." She took the file and tried to file any part of a fingernail she could find. "You have got to stop biting your nails."

"Bad habit." I winced when she got skin instead of nail. "Do you know Eloise Sandlewood?"

She pursed her lips together and continued to file and then she slapped the file on the table, causing me to jump.

"I'm telling you, Ann got what she deserved." She snickered and walked over to the muffins. She picked one up and took a big bite out of it.

"I'm not saying she didn't, but I'm trying to figure out how to clear my name." I looked at my palms. "Read my palms."

Between a giggle, her lips trembled. "I wish I could. I can't." Her hands shook as she put the muffin back up to her lips.

"Why?" I stood up, and then took a good look at my palms.

"I can't interfere with a crime. It's a rule."

I was going to have to go home and dig out that rule book that Izzy had given me. There were too many rules to keep up with and I was finding out new ones every single minute. I wondered if Darla had known anything about the rules in the journal. Darla never lived by the rules.

The front door opened and two women came in.

Chandra cleaned the crumbs off her mouth, and cleared her throat. "Welcome to A Cleansing Spirit Spa. Are you having a nice day in Whispering Falls?"

The women and Chandra continued their conversation. I assumed my manicure was over and so was my line of questioning. At least I had something I could tell Oscar in the morning. Petunia and Gerald could be a lead.

Next on the list was Patience. Two Sisters and a Funeral was located on the opposite end of Main Street. Mr. Prince Charming trotted ahead and let out a few meows along the way when someone would say hello to him.

"Hello there." Izzy stood in the entrance of Mystic Lights. Her usual A-Frame skirt was replaced with a cropped pair of skinny black pants, which made her look even taller than she already was. "I hear you are making your rounds around Whispering Falls asking all sorts of questions."

I wasn't sure how to answer her. Did she really hear it or did she do some type of spiritual thingy to see me? No one seemed safe around here, including me.

"You can't blame me." I shrugged. "No one else seems to take being called a murderer seriously."

She planted her long, skinny fingers on her hips. "You need to let Oscar do his job. Plus the council won't be meeting because Gerald is still ill."

"That's funny. He seemed fine a few minutes ago." I slapped my hand over my mouth. *Dang,* I wished my words were muffled from a mouthful of a Ding Dong, but those were all the way back at my house. Izzy's eyes lowered, I continued to cover up my mistake. "I mean, yesterday when he accused me of trying to kill him. He didn't look great, swollen and all, but his mouth sure was working."

"Um, hum." Izzy nodded.

There was no way she was buying my lie. But I had made a promise to myself that I would figure out the clues and then take them to the council myself. After all, who was going to take better care of me than me? No one.

"I better get going." I pointed off into the distance to Mr. Prince Charming. He was already in front of Two Sisters and a Funeral. "I need to catch up to Mr. Prince Charming. Please let me know what the council says."

I waved over my shoulder. I might not be able to read palms, or see into the future, but I had a sneaky suspicion that Izzy knew more than she was letting on.

"Hello?" I walked into the parlor of the funeral home with Mr. Prince Charming at my feet. One rub against the casket and he was out the door. I yelled after him. "Scaredy-cat!"

"What can we do for you?" Constance stood a distance away from me with a scared look in her eye, and Patience was peeking around Constance back. "We are busy."

"Busy." Patience nodded in agreement. Constance shrugged Patience off her. Patience took a step backwards, crossed her arms and scowled at Constance.

I pointed to the casket. "Is that Ann?"

Hmmm. . .I wonder if I looked at her body if something might come to me. . spiritually speaking, that is.

"It is." Constance stood a little taller, and Patience straightened up a bit, though she was still annoyed with Constance. "The funeral won't be for a couple of days. We are trying to find her family from the west coast spiritual village. That is where she was originally from until she opened the Cleansing Spirit Spa with Chandra."

"It is her." Patience's finger made it way around Constance's thick arm and pointed toward the wooden box.

"A Cleansing Spirit? She owned it with Chandra?" I questioned. Why hadn't anyone mentioned that?

"She was an amazing palm reader." Patience rolled up on her toes and a giddy smile formed across her face.

It seemed that there were so many secrets around here and it was hard trying to keep them straight. I was sure Oscar didn't know that little tidbit of information. It was something else to put on my list to ask Izzy.

"Patience, go get the delivery." Constance waved her hand in the air.

"Delivery!" A man walked through the door with a bouquet of flowers.

Patience scurried off to retrieve the flowers.

"How did you know you were getting a delivery?" I realized I had no clue what their spiritual gift was. Around here, asking was the only way someone was going to tell you something.

"I had a feeling." She folded her hands in front of her. "Now, June Heal, why did you say you were here?"

I ran my hand down Ann's wooden box. If they thought I was the killer, I might as well act as strange as they were. "I didn't tell you why I'm here. But I want to ask a few questions about the autopsy."

"Isn't that Oscar's job?" Constance stood firm. "I'll have the results to him by tomorrow. Then he can answer your questions if he wants to."

She turned around and met Patience at the doorway leading into the part of the funeral home that was off limits to the public. Patience clasped her hands and looked back over her shoulder. We made eye contact. For some reason, I had a feeling that if I got Patience alone, she'd sing like a canary.

I hurried back to the shop. The mojo bags seemed to be a big hit and Patience would be the type that would love one. Especially if I could tell her it would protect her.

I quickly added a few good luck items in one of the makeshift bags before I grabbed my cement foot print and headed home. There were a couple of hours to kill before I made my way back to pay Patience a visit, giving me enough time to read a little more of.

Mr. Prince Charming was on the front porch when I got home.

"There you are." I rubbed my hands down his back which was warm from the sun. "I can't believe you were scared of the Karima sisters."

The sun felt so good that I went inside and grabbed Darla's journal off the side table and a Ding Dong on the way out the door to sit next to Mr. Prince Charming.

I flipped open the journal. I wanted to know more about Darla and her days in Whispering Falls. Maybe it could shed some light on how I could embrace this crazy village.

Otto questioned if I had been hanging out with Eloise. I told him the truth. He was angry at first that I had been keeping this secret from him for so long. He knew something was up because A Dose of Darla has been thriving. He knew the remedies that I had made weren't as potent as the ones being sold in the shop.

Eloise is a dear friend. June loves it there. She is so good while we are working. She doesn't bother anyone there. Otto warned me to be careful. He said that he can't protect us outside of the village, and to keep June in the village.

"Keep me in the village?" That seemed odd since she moved me out of the village after my dad died. Plus my curiosity was up. Who outside of the village did he fear would hurt us?

Meow, meow. Mr. Prince Charming batted at the dangling charms when I turned the page. I pushed him away, but he only came back and batted at my fingers for pushing him.

"Testy little guy." By his purring, I could tell he enjoyed the under-the-chin scratching I was giving him. There was no way I was going to be able to read anymore of Darla's diary with his persistence.

"Stop." I shoved him one last time before I gave up and went into the kitchen to get him a treat.

I looked out the window, over Whispering Falls. Bella was right. Her house had the best view. From a distance, I could see Constance Karima rushing down the street toward the police station. There appeared to be a file in her hand, which made me wonder if it was the autopsy file. Still, it gave me time to get Patience alone and ask her questions.

I pulled my phone out of my bag and texted Oscar. *"Stall Constance. I have some information that I want to confirm with Patience...alone!"*

I put my phone back in my bag and headed straight out the door toward Two Sisters and a Funeral.

The door was ajar and I nudged it a little bit to fit through. Ann's casket was still in the middle of the parlor. Seeing it sent chills along my spine.

"Patience?" I called out a couple times before I heard the shuffling of feet. Within a couple minutes she appeared, looking a little confused. "Hi. I noticed you had given me a strange look when I was here earlier and thought you might want to answer a couple of questions."

"I don't think this is a good idea without Constance." She wrung her hands together. "I. . ."

"Really? Hmm. . ." I rubbed my chin. "I thought you were the brains of the two. I guess my intuition isn't that great after all. I shouldn't be a spiritualist." I laughed.

"Oh, I *am* the smart one." She dropped her hands and drummed her fingers on her thigh. "What would you like to ask me?"

"Let's start with Ann. Did she have honey in her system?" I was going to bombard her with another one, but she might break under pressure.

She leaned back and peered out the front door. It was a perfect view of Main Street and if Constance was coming back, we'd be able to see her. "Not the liquid form. But she tested positive for the supplement. We never thought about checking for it until Oscar asked us to."

"Is that what killed her?" This was a big question. If it was, then it would prove that I didn't kill her, but still didn't explain my charm bracelet that was found in her grips. "You know she was allergic to it."

"No. The supplement works different than the actual honey itself. She did have finger marks around her neck, so she was definitely strangled." She looked off into the distance. "It's so strange that a crime hasn't happened here since your dad was murdered."

"What?" That couldn't be true. My father had been killed over twenty-years ago and now that I was a member of the village it had started up again?

"I. . ." she stuttered, "I've said too much, just like I told Oscar about his parents living here." Her mouth flew open and she raised her hands to cover her mouth.

"Oscar's parents are spiritualists?" I was more confused than before. Izzy never said a word about Oscar's family and Oscar had never mentioned anything about it.

I recalled our conversation during the smudging ceremony and how he had stood back from the crowd. Plus he told me that no one was talking to him when he asked questions. If Oscar wasn't going to give me answer, Uncle Jordan just might. Was he a spiritualist?

"How do you like living in your parent's house?" Patience changed the subject.

"My parent's house?" I looked up the hill and could see the little cottage perfectly. "That's Bella's."

"Oh, dear." Patience patted the sides of her short hair down with her finger tips. "I really have to go and work.

Please don't tell anyone you talked to me or Constance will be mad at me."

"One more, please?" I put my hands together and begged. "What is your spiritual gift?"

It was a legitimate question.

"Oh," Her eyebrows raised and color came into her cheeks, "we help spirits find the light."

She scurried off to the back of the funeral home before I could ask any more questions. I had come here to find out about Ann, but left with a lot more questions.

My phone beeped from deep down in my bag. I pulled the strap from around my shoulder and dug through it. I pulled it out and there was a text from Oscar. *Sorry, she's in a hurry. I need to talk to you when you are done.*

"I bet you do," I muttered and looked in the direction of the police station. Something wasn't adding up.

The streets were crowded with visitors. I weaved in and out of them to get home, only to run smack dab into Gerald.

He placed his top hat on his head, and with a swift pat, it covered his forehead. "June." He nodded.

"What?" There was a slight sarcasm to my tone. I was done with being nice. After all, he had accused me of trying to kill him, when he was the one with more motive than me.

"Who are you off to kill today?" His masterful expression of distaste shone through.

There was no way he was still mad. Didn't he worry that I was going to go before the council and tell them about his little rendezvous with Petunia?

"How's Petunia?" I asked, trying to get his goat.

"Now!" He shook his finger in my face. Of course it had to be right in front of A Cleansing Spirit Spa. Chandra didn't miss a thing. Although I couldn't see her, I could see the tip of her turban peeking around the door. "You leave her out of it. This is between you and me! I told them you were nothing like Otto."

"Whatever old man! If I wanted you dead, I'd have done more than just blow a little cedar smoke your way." I huffed back at him. Instantly I knew that I shouldn't have said that, but I was tired of people talking about my family.

"You hoo!" Chandra giggled from the entrance of the spa. "You two okay?"

"Fine," I said as I stomped down the street toward the police station.

There was no time to see Oscar. I wondered how well I did know him. Really I had no idea what his police duties had ever been, here or in Locust Grove. We just hung out together. Which made me wonder if he knew all along that we were spiritualists, and for some reason was keeping it from me?

Chapter Seventeen

"Come on." I called for Mr. Prince Charming after I made it back to the house to get my keys to the Green Machine. "Let's go to Locust Grove."

Mewl. Mr. Prince Charming was curled up on the sofa where the stream of sunlight warmed it.

"Hmm." I sighed. He had become less active since we moved to Whispering Falls. In Locust Grove he was always on top of me, following me everywhere. I didn't know his real age, and wondered if he was getting old.

I didn't have time to waste, so I let him stay behind while I hopped in the Green Machine and drove back into Locust Grove.

I parked in the driveway of the old Cape Cod. Someone had cut the grass, but it still looked to be the same…a little in shambles. Which made me question if I was really living in my parent's house in Whispering Falls. Darla didn't seem to be the same person she was in Whispering Falls. The house was certainly not the same.

Jordan Park's police cruiser wasn't in the driveway. My intuition told me not to do it, but I did anyway. Before I could stop myself, I had used the spare key under the porcupine shoe cleaner on the front porch of Jordan's house and let myself in. After all, he did say he was going to have me over for lasagna.

Even if he did come home, he wouldn't find it odd that I would be sitting on the couch watching TV. Many times he'd come home to find me vegged out while Darla was at the flea market or if I went to church with them, I'd hang out afterwards.

But I was on a mission to find anything out I could about Oscar's family. We really didn't discuss his family much when we were kids. They were already dead when we moved according to Darla's journal, but I was too young to remember. I couldn't even recall seeing a picture of his parents or him when he was little.

The house was like it always was. Simple. That was one thing I loved about hanging out with Oscar and his Uncle. There were no smells of ingredients, everything was always picked up and put in its place. Not like home with

Darla. There was food all over the kitchen, the house reeked of cures, and clothes were everywhere.

I scoured the book shelves in the family room looking for a photo album. There were books, but no albums. Hmmm. . ."Living spiritually." I pulled the book off the shelf.

I flipped the pages to get a glance of what this might be about and a picture fell out. The black and white photo was old. I could tell by the clothing and the two little boys standing by tricycles. The man and woman had their arms around each other, which made me believe they were the parents of the two boys. By instinct, I stuck the photo in my pocket and put the book back.

There wasn't anything there to help me. I walked back into Oscar's room and found it funny that I had only been in his room one other time. After I told Darla that I had gone in there, she forbade me to ever step foot in a boy's room again. And I listened.

It was exactly like I remembered it. The twin bed was made with a baseball comforter and baseball trophies lined the wall. I had forgotten about all Oscar's baseball games I went to with him and his Uncle.

I slide the closest doors open. The balls on the track made a screech like they hadn't been opened in a long time. A few clothing items hung on hangers, and a few boxes of different memorabilia sat on the top shelf, but nothing stood out to me.

With my hands planted on my hips I looked around the room. Had I let my thoughts make me crazy into believing that Oscar could be behind all of this? Not necessarily the murders, but did he know about us being spiritual and that's why he was my friend and when given the opportunity suggested we move to Whispering Falls? It was awfully convenient that he, by chance, had driven into Whispering Falls.

And it wouldn't be the first time Oscar Park talked me into anything.

I snapped my fingers. *The bed.* I got down on the floor. I use to shove stuff under my bed all the time. It was dark under there. I plunged my hand in my bag, and felt around for the phone. I pulled it out, opened it, and used it as a light. There was a small plastic container with a lid far in the back. I swiveled my body on the floor and shimmied under the bed. With the box in my grip, I pulled myself out from underneath and stood up. The entire front of my clothes was covered in dust bunnies.

"Eeck!" I screamed and the box and all its contents flew into the air. Mr. Prince Charming stood on top the bed as if he was there the entire time. "Mr. Prince Charming! You scared me."

I continued to brush the dust off myself and wondered how he got there, like I had wondered so many times before.

"What are you doing here?" I picked up the box and sat down on the bed next to the cat. "More importantly, how did you get here?"

One of these days, I was going to have to take a day and follow him around, unless I was in jail.

Meow, meow. He nudged my arm with his head like he was asking for forgiveness.

I rubbed him. "You are so smart. Okay. Let's see what's in here." I put the box in my lap and took the lid off.

There were a couple different looking dolls in it. I picked the one with the brown yarn hair up and looked at it. The doll was stuffed with hay and the fabric of the clothing resembled that of a woman. Its yarn hair was long and it wore a hat that looked like a makeshift turban.

"Owww. . ." I dropped the doll when something poked my finger. With my finger stuck in my mouth, I picked the doll up off the floor and turned it over. There were stick pins stuck in the back of the doll. "What the hell?"

Hiss, Hiss. Mr. Prince Charming jumped off the bed. I looked out the window and Jordan was standing in front of the Cape Cod. He looked like he was checking out the Green Machine. I quickly grabbed the other doll and shoved them in the waist of my jeans and pulled my top down to cover them.

I ran into the family room and grabbed the magazine off the table. Mr. Prince Charming was gone. I didn't have to worry about him. He could take care of himself.

"Hello there." Jordan walked into the door. "I was going to walk over to your house. I saw your car over there."

"I just got here and I helped myself to the spare key." I pointed toward the coffee table where I put the key. "And just thought I'd wait."

"And read A Cop's World Magazine?" His brows dipped.

"Um," I closed the magazine and looked at the front. *Idiot.* "I don't smell any lasagna."

"I didn't know you were coming over, but I'm sure I can whip something up." He took his holster off and sat it in the chair. He walked into the kitchen and opened the refrigerator like he was trying to find something to fix. "Is Oscar coming?"

"No." I followed him and grabbed a handful of grapes off the vine that was sitting on the kitchen counter. "I really came here to ask you a few questions about my dad."

Slowly he shut the refrigerator door. Standing there with his hand on the handle, he just stared at it. I stood behind him waiting for his answer, but he stood in silence.

"I mean, everyone told me that he and you were responding to a routine speeding stop and it went wrong. The guy pulled out a gun and fired two shots. One at your gut and one at my dad's chest." I recalled everything that Darla had told me, there was never a reason to question it until now. My entire existence had been a lie up until a few days ago, and I couldn't help but hear Patience's words about 'no other crime' since my father died. And if my father died in Whispering Falls, which all of Darla's journal entries say, then how did Jordan know my dad?

"I see that you've been snooping around." His voice was jittery.

"No, I've been sitting on your couch." Oh, my. Feat knotted inside my stomach. Did he know that I took those funny looking dolls?

"Not here, June. Whispering Falls." He placed both hands on the counter and took in a deep breath. "I was afraid this was going to happen."

He stood up and shook his head.

"Please tell me. I'm accused of murder, and everything I know up until now has all been a lie." I begged.

He pulled up his shirt and the scar from the gunshot wound was visible. He pointed to it. "I did get this from a routine traffic stop. But I didn't know your father." He took his holster out of the chair and sat it on the floor. He sat down. "When Darla moved in I felt sorry for you girls. It was just me and Oscar up until then, so I made sure I kept an eye out on you two. After awhile she started to open up about how you guys lived in a village and that your father had gotten killed. I didn't ask any questions."

"Did you know it was Whispering Falls?" I asked. Tears hung on to the bottom rim of my eye lids.

"No, not until the other day when I went to visit with Oscar and I saw the sign. Darla told me that she owned an herb shop." He put his hands in his lap. "I put two and two together, like a good cop. The only thing that bothers me is that there are two unsolved crimes. Your father's and now this other woman."

"Ann." I cringed. The pins from the dolls were beginning to stick me. I made my way to the door. "I better go. I think Oscar got the autopsy report back and I want to see if there is anything that will point the finger at someone else."

Jordan followed behind me with the spare key in his hand and opened the door.

"Oscar has told me a few things and I'm going to help out as much as I can without getting into trouble." He handed me the key to put back under the porcupine shoe cleaner. "You promise you will let me know if I can help you."

I put my Girl Scout fingers in the air. "I promise."

Chapter Eighteen

Nothing made sense. I looked over at the strange dolls in the passenger seat of the Green Machine. Things were getting more complicated by the minute.

Oscar seemed awfully suspicious but my intuition said "no way." I couldn't discount the nagging feeling that Oscar wasn't doing all he could to help solve Ann's murder. Not to mention he didn't keep Constance busy while I asked Patience a few questions. The Oscar that lived in Locust Grove did everything he could to keep me safe.

Unfortunately, I was not feeling so safe.

I couldn't forget what Patience had said about Oscar's parents being spiritualists. *Hmmm. . .how* convenient it was for Oscar to talk me into moving to Whispering Falls.

And now these. I picked one of the dolls up. All sorts of questions formed in my head, but I wasn't sure if I could trust Oscar at this point to even ask him about them.

Putting the doll back on the seat, I leaned a little more and flipped the glove box open. I patted around until I found what I was looking for.

Ding Dong. I pulled it out from my secret stash and just for a moment, the chocolate goodness made everything feel like it was going to be okay.

That went away as soon as I pulled into Whispering Falls and Oscar was standing on the porch. I slipped the dolls into the glove box and slammed it shut.

"Seriously, June?" Oscar scratched his head. "Why can't you leave solving crimes to the professionals? Uncle Jordan called to tell me you are all worried. And you should be, but I'm doing everything I can. I promise."

A little leery, I chose my words carefully, "You don't seem to be doing anything to help, so I have to do it myself." I unlocked the door. My eyes narrowed when I saw Mr. Prince Charming sitting in the couch in the sunlight, like he never left. But we both knew better. Oscar followed me in. "You, yourself even said that no one is talking to you."

"We might live among spiritualists, but there are rules that have to be followed like in every other city." He sat down on the couch and Mr. Prince Charming jumped down. "Why does that cat hate me?"

I shrugged and picked Mr. Prince Charming up, giving him a little love. I was beginning to wonder the same thing. From what I understood, animals had great instincts and could really sense someone that was bad. Mr. Prince Charming didn't think Jordan was bad, did he?

"Why did you go see Uncle Jordan? I'm the cop here." He had an annoyance in his voice.

"I wanted him to talk to you about getting this case solved." I lied. There was really no need to tell Oscar about my dad's death. That would open a whole new can of worms. "Didn't he tell you why I was there?"

"Just that you were looking around and trying to solve Ann's murder." He stood up and walked back to the door. "I got Ann's autopsy back and I'm going to go over it with the council before I can share anything with you."

"Fine." I shut the door behind him. I wasn't too worried about the council, I wanted to know why Jordan didn't tell Oscar that I wanted to know about my dad or that I had found out that my dad wasn't with Jordan when he was shot, and that Jordan met us when we moved to Locust Grove.

I took the two concrete foot prints out of the pantry where I had stored them. They had the exact same ridges.

I drummed my fingers on Darla's journal that was sitting on the kitchen counter. There had to be something there. Something concrete for me to go on. Surely there had to be some advice. Something more than 'follow your instincts' because my instincts were proving to be leading me in the wrong direction.

I went over the clues about Gerald and Petunia's little secret with Ann; Chandra and Ann's business partnership going up in flames and Izzy's resentment towards Ann because she had to take her in. Not to mention all the stuff Petunia told me about my family and Oscar's. And then there was Oscar. His lack of gathering clues, not to mention the funny dolls, were adding up to the fact that Oscar knew more about this village before we moved here than he'd let on.

I sat on the couch and opened up the journal.

"I don't like the feeling of always being watched. No matter where I go or what I do, they always tell Otto. I have no friends. Only Eloise, and even she if off limits."

Turn over, turn over. The hands curled around the neck. *No!* I searched the scene for any more clues like Oscar had asked me to do, but it was difficult to stop from trying to see who the victim was. *Focus, June. Focus.* I didn't care about the victim as much as I wanted a new clue to who this killer was.

My heart sank to my stomach as the hands peeled away. The sun trickled into the depths of the water and focused on the space between the thumb and the forefinger. *What is that?* The sun got brighter. *A mole? Man hands?*

Quickly I jumped out of bed.

"Let's go for a walk." I motioned for the cat. It was time to visit Eloise. She helped Darla, surely she'd be up for helping me. I grabbed the dolls. For some reason, my intuition told me to take them.

Chapter Nineteen

Eloise said it was in the clearing beyond the wood.

Mr. Prince Charming was all over going for a walk. He trotted ahead of me leading me straight toward the big rock as if he knew exactly where we were going.

The smudging bundles were still lying next to the big rock, which I found very odd. If Gerald was accusing me of trying to murder him, I would have thought Oscar would have come up here to get the bundle of the remaining cedar.

I set the dolls on the rock and gathered the bundles into a pile next to the rock. In the back of my mind, I couldn't help but think that this was definitely negligence on Oscar's part. This only added to my suspicions that Oscar was somehow involved.

I glanced at the dolls. The rock illuminated around them. I grabbed them and pulled away when the heat coming off them was steaming up the air. I picked up the bundle closest to me and took the dolls off the rock. Immediately the rock went back to being a rock and the bundle smoked.

I fanned it to put it out, only it created more smoke.

Hiss, hiss. Mr. Prince Charming ran in the opposite direction.

"What? I'm trying!" I yelled after him, throwing the bundle on the ground and stomping it out with my shoe. "I hope that wasn't the cedar one." I looked at the charred remains. The last thing I needed was for Gerald to have another reaction. "What was that?"

Something in the opposite direction of where the cat had run moved behind a tree.

"Is somebody there?" I yelled in the direction, but nothing moved or came forward. I shrugged it off to something else that didn't make sense in Whispering Falls, and grabbed the dolls.

Mewl, mewl. The cat sat on the edge of the woods dragging his tail along the grass.

"Fine. I'll follow you." I looked at the pile of smudging bundles to make sure nothing else as going to catch fire, and made a mental note to grab them on my way back.

The further we walked, the foggier it got, and the more I realized that Mr. Prince Charming had no clue where to go and my instincts weren't giving me any hunches.

Just when I was about to turn around, something caught my eye.

Wow. Between a couple of trees, there was a platform built high off the ground and on the platform was a two-story house. The wooden stairs led up to a cozy wrap-around porch. I tried to see if there were any lights on, which I should've seen through the fog, but it didn't appear that anyone was there.

This had to be Eloise's house. No wonder Darla loved it here. But why would she live all the way out here?

I walked around the side. Lanterns hung from the tree dotted the fog and shone enough for me to see the gravel pathway. It was hard to concentrate on where it led with all the beautiful flowers that were planted on both sides. I ran my hand along the vibrant purple, green, red, orange, and yellow flowers. Wisteria vines provided a canopy leading to a clearing. It reminded me of the beautiful vine that covered the overhang of the front of A Dose of Darla.

I blinked. I blinked harder. My heart raced as though it was going to leap right out of my chest. Rows and rows of herbs were neatly planted and proportioned perfectly. All I could see was Mr. Prince Charming's tail waving above the rows as he darted in and out of the herbs.

Each row had a painted wood sign with the names of the herbs that followed in line. Herbs I had never heard of. I walked in front of each row, touching each herb sign.

"Rose petals, moonflower, mandrake root, seaweed, shrinking violet, dream dust, fairy dust, magic peanut, lucky clover, steal rose," I whispered. "Spooky shroom?"

What in the world where all of these used for?

"I wondered how long it was going to take you to find me." Eloise popped up. Her short red hair glistened from the ray of sunshine peeking through the fog. "I'm just picking some Wolfsbane. It snaps off the vine much better with the fog." She held the orange furry plant in the air.

Wolfsbane? I wasn't going to question it.

She stood up and with her arms straight out and her head tilted back, she inhaled deeply and slowly exhaled. "I love foggy mornings. Well?" She cocked her head to the side with a question in her eyes.

"Well what?" I wasn't sure if I was supposed to apologize for trespassing or Mr. Prince Charming batting at the little creatures flying in the air. I scolded him, "Stop it!"

"Are you ready to eat?" She gestured toward the opposite end of the garden to a gazebo with twinkling lights twisted around the wooden spindles. In the center was a table covered in a yellow cloth, and a place setting for two.

I guess she had been expecting me.

"How did you know I was coming?" Tension crept in my shoulders. I reached back and kneaded it before I walked toward the gazebo.

Eloise glanced over her shoulder and laughed. There was a spark in her eye. She threw the Wolfsbane into a simmering pot and stirred it before she came to join me.

"Let's say that I can see into the future," She folded her hands in front of her. "Most of the time. Plus I figured you had a lot of questions and eventually my name was going to come up."

I sat on the rickety chair and carefully scooted myself up to the table. There were so many different options to choose from, I didn't know what to eat first. The assortment of scones, fruits, quiches, and a Ding Dong.

"These are my favorite." I picked up the Ding Dong and peeled back the foil wrapper.

"Your mom told me." She ate one too. "Your mom visited me one time after she moved and told me that you had discovered artificial foods like Ding Dongs." She leaned forward and whispered, "Your mother loved them too." A smile crossed her face. She knew she had just told me a big secret. "I'm sure you have a lot of questions."

She was right. I did. And there was no beating around the bush.

"Exactly how did you meet my mom?" I looked around the scones and picked out a blueberry one with a lot of powdered sugar on top.

"Darla was an unusual one. She had agreed to live in the village when she married Otto. He wanted to serve the place where he grew up. Only she wasn't a spiritualist, which was good because that meant she could open her own shop." Eloise rearranged the droopy flowers in the center of the table. They sprang to life from her touch. She brushed her hands together. "Her homeopathic store wasn't doing well, and I had just been banned from the village. It was a win situation for both of us."

"What do you mean?" I reached out to touch a flower sitting on the table. Eloise took it before I touched it and put it in the vase with the other vibrant flowers.

"Darla loved homeopathic medicine. People come here to seek true remedies that make them feel better. That is what Whispering Falls provides for all those visitors. They leave feeling great." She picked up the pink tea server and poured some in each cup. "Darla was straight homeopathic with no little extra . . .um. . .feel good."

"Feel good?" Darla told many of her customers at the flea market that it took a few weeks for the homeopathic cure to take effect.

"My potions are instant. That is what needed to be sold in A Dose of Darla so we made a pact. She could use my potions to help in her remedies in exchange to visit me. The only person who knew about it was Izzy. She knew Darla's cures had gotten a little extra added in and knew Darla didn't do it on her own."

"And in the end, you two became best friends?" It made a lot of sense. "The recipe book that she used is yours?"

"It is. When your father was murdered, she had to leave the village for her safety. She had you to raise so I gave her my book." She looked out into her garden. "I haven't had any friends since I was banned."

"Murdered?" I recalled Patience calling my dad's death a crime, but not murder. "I thought he was killed through a crime gone bad."

"Here, have a few berries." She shoved the bowl in my face.

"According to some of the spiritualists. . ."

She wasn't going to answer that, so I filed it in the back of my head and continued with my questions she might answer. "Why were you banned?"

Her eyes stared at me. I tried not to give a reaction. "I'm from a village out west that allows inter-spiritual relationships. Very common. They found out that I was mixed and told me I couldn't live there so I created my own little world here." Her hands swept in front of her.

"So you aren't a full-spiritualist?" This whole other world was something I only thought lived in children's stories.

"I'm a Fairiwick." She held her hands together and blew across them. Golden sprinkles filled the air and floated down, covering the ground as daisies. "I'm part fairy, part spiritualist. My mother was a fairy, my father was a homeopathic potion maker."

"I. . ." I struggled to understand what she was saying.

"Really my dad was part Warlock part potion maker, but in my village we all were sorta like. . ." she hesitated and then walked over to the cauldron. Slowly she mixed the bubbling mixture with the paddle. Green smoke hovered over the golden pot. She continued, "A mix of things. And that is something Whispering Falls doesn't allow."

"That isn't right." Once I got my name cleared, I was going to go in front of the council and ask them about this.

"It might not be right. But is anything?" She put her hand in the air. A little mound of dust formed on her hand. She tossed it in the cauldron. Her cloak swished as she made her way back to her seat. "How did you figure out you have your dad's talent?"

Talent? I wasn't sure what she was talking about. I didn't know my dad's talent, just that he was part of this village.

"I had never questioned what he had done. I just assumed he was a cop all his life. My best friend, Oscar Park, told me about Whispering Falls. And Izzy found me." I knew not to listen to Oscar. I shook my head. "I should've stayed in Locust Grove."

Her chair went crashing to the floor when she stood up. "Did you say Oscar Park?"

I nodded. "Yes, he's the new police officer of Whispering Falls."

Nervously she walked down the gazebo steps. She turned around when she reached the bottom one. "It was good chatting with you. We must do it again." She glided on the gravel path toward her house.

"Wait!" I ran behind her trying to catch up. There were so many more questions I needed answered. When I reached the bottom steps of her porch, I took the dolls out of my waist band. I held one in each hand and held them high above my head. "What are these?"

Slowly she turned around and her eyes darted back and forth between my hands. She darted down the steps just as a clap of thunder echoed throughout the woods and into the crystal clear blue sky.

I fell to the ground and laid in fetal position. "Please don't kill me," I begged.

Damn! I've got to stop listening to my intuition or I wouldn't be begging for my life.

"Where did you get these?" She snapped them out of my hands. "Whose voodoo dolls are these?" Her shadow towered over me.

"You aren't going to kill me are you?" I looked up.

"No, get up." She held the dolls in one hand and stuck out the other. I took it and she helped me up. "I haven't seen voodoo dolls in a long time. Especially ones that have pins stuck in them and are personalized."

She pointed to the yarned thread on the back of the one doll that looked like a woman. It was a makeshift "D."

"Darla?" I questioned hoping I was wrong. Had Oscar really hated my family that much?

"I'm afraid so. I'm afraid she was murdered." A single tear fell down Eloise's cheek. "Did you get this from Oscar Park?" Her voice was low and steady.

"I found them under his bed."

"I'm Oscar's aunt. I moved here to find him. I was afraid this was going to happen." Her mouth turned down. "My sister was married to Oscar's father. She was a witch. I heard they were moving here, and then they disappeared."

"What about Uncle Jordan?"

"Who is Jordan?" She pulled back, looking confused. "I don't have a brother."

"Oscar lived in Locust Grove and was raised by his Uncle Jordan. Oscar told me that his parent's were moving here and were killed in a car accident." I had to get some answers from Jordan. I was beginning to get a craving for lasagna. "That's when he went to live with his Uncle Jordan."

"I've spent all my life looking for Oscar. We couldn't find him." She held the dolls in her hands, she rubbed them. "I was afraid of this. If a child was raised by a non-spiritualist, most of the kids become angry and don't understand their powers. Oscar was in line to become a sorcerer." She took the pins out of the doll. "I'm afraid these are a sign of an evil sorcerer."

She plopped down on the step and I sat next to her.

"A murder in the village is just like an evil spirit." She put her head in her hands.

"Did you say evil spirit?" Madame Torres popped into my head. Was Oscar who she was talking about? There was no way Oscar knew that he was a sorcerer or even spiritual.

Eloise nodded. The fear was deep-set in her eyes.

"Why would Oscar want to hurt me or anyone else in the village?" Did Oscar sit in his room and poke holes in the dolls? What did have against Darla? None of this made sense. Hell, for that matter, nothing in this entire spiritual village made sense.

"Am I in trouble?" I spent the next hour telling her about my nightmares and how Oscar knew everything about me. I told her about all my suspicions about who had motives to kill Ann and what the evidence was. That included Gerald, Petunia, Izzy, and even Oscar.

She gave a tilted smile, leaving room for the worry lines that had formed around her eyes. "Go about your business for now. I need to cleanse your house. I will have to wait until the first break of dawn. People can't see me then."

"Is that why you were cleansing the streets in the early morning?" I recalled seeing her and Izzy.

"Yes." Slowly she ascended up her steps. She turned back around and pointed toward my wrist. "Never take that off."

"Don't worry." I twirled the bracelet around my wrist. Mr. Prince Charming did figure eights around my ankles. "I need all the protection I can get."

It was time for my lasagna dinner. There were questions I needed answered and I wasn't going to ask Oscar.

Chapter Twenty

I made it out of the woods without getting lost or killed. Mr. Prince Charming was nowhere to be found. I circled around the big rock to pick up the bundles, but they were gone. I could've sworn I left them next to the rock. There was no time to investigate where the bundles had gone. They probably blew away.

Once I reached the house, I called Jordan and told him I'd be there at six, which gave me plenty of time to go visit Izzy.

Mystic Lights was busy and Izzy waved, motioning me to her office in the back of the shop. She'd be back when she was finished.

I sat in the chair in front of her desk. There was a faint glow coming through the crack on the bottom of the door. *Squeak*, the chair groaned as I leaned back and looked into the shop. The glow was calling me, or so my intuition said, or maybe curiosity, but I wanted to make sure that Izzy was busy and wouldn't notice me snooping around. After all, I had to figure out who killed Ann, because I knew it wasn't me.

I tiptoed over to the closest and slowly turned the knob. As the door opened, the glow got brighter. And once my eyes adjusted, the crystal ball illuminated with all yellow, red, orange, and purple lines. The lines parted and a face appeared. The eyes were gaunt, the lips were rosy red, and the skin was pale.

"Hello, June. I've been waiting for you." Madame Torres' green eyes were no longer hollow, and the red medusa hair flowed beyond the boundaries of the glass ball. The vision made my heart pound and my skin crawl with fright. There was no mistake, she had definitely been looking for me.

"Don't be scared, dear. I'm here to help." Her voice lowered, her eyes darkened showing her power.

I fiddled with my charm bracelet. *Right now would be a good time for the dog charm to kick in.* I knew nothing about crystal balls. There was no time to let evil in my life.

"Yes. You are in grave danger."

No joke, tell me something I didn't know or dream about.

"Do not take any remedies for nightmares or it could cost you your life. The village needs you." She spoke softly and swiftly. "You must not trust. . ."

The ball went black.

Clink, clink. I knew that sound from Izzy's heels. The shoes filled the silence in the air. I grabbed the crystal ball.

"What are you doing?" Madame Torres voice was demanding. "Put me down!"

Without a word, I checked all the doors. Damn! Closet. I shut the door. Click, click. Izzy was getting closer. Please help me find a way out, I prayed opening the last door. The steps to the cellar looked scarier going down then it had that day when I was looking up.

"Shh!" I held the ball close to my eyes so she knew I meant business. "You're going with me."

"You're making me sick with all this rolling around." She wasn't going to be quiet.

I put her in my bag with the rest of my stuff, including the voodoo dolls.

"Wait! I'm scared of the dark!" She screamed before I shut the flap. "Who's voodoo dolls are these?"

I rushed down the steps into the cellar. I knew the way out from when I was in there before the smudging ceremony. I pushed the doors open leading to the back of the building. There was no time to waste. Izzy was going to know that I took the ball and left out the cellar, so there was no sense in shutting the doors again.

There was no sense in coming back to Whispering Falls until Ann's murder was solved. I knew exactly what I needed to do and it included Uncle Jordan.

Chapter Twenty One

I ran as fast as I could to my cottage. There was no time to waste. I had to get out of Whispering Falls until my plan was in the works.

I didn't even turn around to see if Izzy was following me.

"Mr. Prince Charming?" I hollered throughout the house when I got there. Of course he was nowhere to be found. He would find me. That was one thing I could count on. I grabbed my keys and Darla's journal off the counter and hopped in the Green Machine.

The tires squealed. I was out of there.

I had a couple hours before I was going to Uncle Jordan's for dinner. With one hand on the wheel and the other stuck in my bag, I felt around for my phone.

"Left, left," Madame Torres called out from my purse. "The phone is to the left!"

She was right. I found the phone and called Jordan.

"June, what's going on?" Jordan didn't bother to beat around the bush. "Oscar called looking for you."

"Did you tell him I was coming for dinner?" I needed to get Uncle Jordan's help without Oscar knowing.

"No, I didn't. I figured I'd give you a chance to tell me why you are running?" There was concern in his voice. "Oscar said that you had stolen something from one of the merchants and that you left Whispering Falls when one of the laws clearly states that if you are accused of a crime you aren't allowed to leave the village."

"I know it sounds like I'm guilty, but I need your help. If I'm wrong, then you can turn me in to Oscar." I pleaded for him to help me.

"Okay. And the only reason is because I care about your family. You are like one of my own. I will continue to tell Oscar that I haven't heard from you." He sighed. "I don't get off work for another couple of hours. Go on to the house and I'll be there soon."

"Thank you, Jordan." He was my last hope. I had to get him to agree with my plan.

"You're welcome. You can pop the lasagna in the oven. I made it last night. It's in the refrigerator." He had comfort in his words.

I hung up the phone and put it back in my bag.

"I hate the dark!" Madame Torres hollered when I slipped the phone in. I would deal with her once I got to Jordan's house.

I peered in my rear-view mirror the entire time. I made sure no one from Whispering Falls had followed me.

The old Cape Cod looked lonely across the street from Jordan's. Or maybe it was me that was lonely for it. I turned the Green Machine off and took out Madame Torres.

"Pshew." Her glow had gone from green to crystal blue. "Thank you for getting me out of there. Those voodoo dolls are evil, evil I tell you!"

"Now that I have you in my hands, I need you to tell me who to stay away from." The ball turned a flaming red.

Madame Torres' eyes deepened into a dark green, almost black, her face paled, her lips flamed. "You have possession of me illegally. I'm just another spiritualist to you. By law of the village, I cannot read you." The ball went black and she disappeared.

I shook it.

"What? Illegal?" I waited to see if she was going to come back. I shook it a couple more times, but nothing seemed to happen. I set the ball underneath the seat and grabbed my bag.

Uncle Jordan was going to be another hour. I got the spare key from underneath the porcupine shoe cleaner and let myself in.

There were so many questions I wanted to ask him. Especially the ones about Oscar being a sorcerer, which meant that Jordan had to be a spiritualist of some sort.

Exhausted, I sat down on the couch. It wasn't long until I heard a scratch at the door. Without having to think about it, I knew it was Mr. Prince Charming.

"Hey, buddy." I opened the door. "Do you miss Locust Grove as much as I do?"

He turned to look out the door and we both stood there staring at the ole Cape Cod.

"Come on." I shut the door behind his wagging tail. He followed me into the kitchen and watched as I turned on the oven and put the lasagna in.

We made ourselves comfortable on the couch to wait for the oven timer to go off. Mr. Prince Charming was nestled in my lap. I took the journal out of my bag.

"Today at the shop, Ann asked me if I wanted a free manicure. Of course I said yes. It would be a treat after a long day of work, only it wasn't. She asked all sorts of questions about how we feel about June not being a spiritualist. Then she had the nerve to tell me that our life was going to dramatically change, ending it by saying, "poor June." Well, I better stop writing. Otto has gone to work and I'm very excited about going to see Eloise. She has a new potion for growing hair. I can just see Gerald now with a full head of hair sticking out of that top hat. Makes me laugh every time. Plus Mac is going to take June for some fishing at the lake. She loves spending time with him."

*Hmmm. . .*I looked over at Mr. Prince Charming. He didn't seem too fazed by Darla's revelation. I read it aloud, "poor June." What did Ann mean? Too bad she was dead or I'd be able to ask her.

Was she referring to the upcoming death of my dad? Was she trying to tell Darla about it? Or was she talking about us moving to Locust Grove? Either way, I was probably never going to know unless Darla wrote it in her journal?

Before I knew it, I was fast asleep.

Turn over, turn over! Save yourself! I watched the victim do something that Ann nor Gerald did. The victim's hands lifted, and struggled with the killer. I watched helplessly as the struggle continued. Then all of a sudden I saw it. The dog charm and Celtic knot were flailing around in the water as the victim struggled. *NO!*

Me! The victim was me!

Fear gripped my insides as I propelled myself out of slumber. I had to do something. This time I was dreaming my own fate. And now fate was in my hands. The crystal ball was right. There was no way I was going to take a remedy to stop my nightmares.

"I could smell that lasagna from outside." Jordan unhooked his holster and sat it on the table just inside the door.

"How do you think we feel? Our mouths have been watering." I hugged him. Mr. Prince Charming didn't bother getting up. "Thanks for having me."

Steam exploded from the deep dish when he cut into it.

"I. . .um. . .I know I put you in a compromising position." I grabbed my plate and took it to the table. I pulled the chair out and sat down without making eye contact. "I don't want you to pick between me and Oscar. He is really your family. Plus you are a cop, but I really need your help. And you need to keep it from Oscar."

"Oh." Jordan sat across the table and had a curious stare. "You two never keep secrets."

"I know, but I think it's a fine line between murder suspect and friend."

"I don't like keeping secrets." He patted the badge on his uniform. "Part of the job, but I'm listening."

"You know I have those nightmares. Well, I dreamed about Ann's murder before it had happened. Only I didn't know it was her." I left out the fact that I saw a mole on the killer's hand. "The dreams are becoming more vivid."

"So you are a spiritualist." He put his fork on his plate and waited for my answer.

My mouth dropped open. So what Eloise had said was true. They *were* spiritualist. "How did you know?"

At this point I only wanted him to help me catch Oscar. I didn't want to accuse Oscar of being an evil spirit or I'd fear Jordan wouldn't help me. After all, I was going to expose Oscar as the killer, so asking him questions about their family was off-limits.

"Oscar told me to combine our cities since Whispering Falls is so small. You aren't going to put some spell on me are you?" He was half joking, half serious.

"I'm not that kind of spiritualist. Supposedly I know how to mix the right ingredients for cures." I pointed in the direction of my Cape Cod. "And we see how that turned out."

I left out the little detail about Ann burning down my shed. I let Jordan think I had done it.

"Are you going to try to combine both communities?" I asked. Oscar never mentioned a meeting with his uncle about combining the two.

Izzy would never let that happen. Hell, the village didn't let in Fairiwicks. They certainly weren't going to allow the mortals.

"Not any time soon. They would have to have a vote and change the laws in place. If you were in Locust Grove and under the suspect umbrella, you'd be out on bond, not just hanging around until they figure it out." He glanced over, but I didn't give a reaction. I knew the law and yes, it was a little suspicious that each of the victims was holding something that tied them to me. Jordan knew his boundaries. "Let's talk about your nightmares."

"Anyway, I had a nightmare that I was the next victim." I swallowed hard trying to digest what I had said out loud. It didn't sound good or sit well in my stomach. I was afraid my lasagna was going to come up, but I needed to eat for strength. I wanted to put my plan in place tonight.

Mewl, mewl. Mr. Prince Charming lay under the table, his tail slowly wagged up and down.

There was fear in Jordan's eyes. "How do you know it's you?"

I held my hand in the air. The charm bracelet dangled. "The difference between dreams is that *I* seem to struggle with the killer. I can see my bracelet."

"Did you tell Oscar all of this?"

"No. He's so busy trying to figure it all out that I thought I could count on you to help me." I lied.

He eyed me suspiciously.

"Okay." I put my hands in the air. "I think it would be a conflict of interest. So I'm asking for your help."

"And what would that be?" He put his elbows on the table and locked his hands together.

"Well, the killer is doing this at night. I figured if I would be at the lake, say at midnight, and you were hiding in the woods, the killer would come to get me and you could tackle them." It seemed pretty simple.

"When did you want to do this?" He didn't seem to act like my request was stupid.

"Midnight. Tonight." I blurted it out before I had time to think about it and change my mind. The sooner the better.

"Tonight?" His eyebrows shot up.

I nodded.

"I don't know, June. It's kind of risky." He took a bite of his bread. "I'm not a citizen and it's not my jurisdiction."

"But you have a gun. It's no different from your stakeout here." There was no way I was going to take no for an answer. It was foolproof. "We can say that you were visiting me. I *have* to get my life back."

"Visiting you at midnight?" He asked. He did have a point.

"If I'm right, you won't have to explain why you were there at midnight." I begged, "Please?"

"Fine. I will be in the woods at midnight." He shook his head. "I will flash a flashlight twice to let you know that I'm there. Do not go out there until you see my flashlight."

"Got it." I took a few bites of my lasagna. I felt a little relieved knowing that my life was about to get back to normal soon. "Can I ask you about my dad?"

Cough, cough. Jordan pulled his napkin up, covering his mouth.

"It's just that I'm beginning to figure out things about my previous life and I don't understand how or why my dad was with you when he got killed." It was a legitimate question. And one that I needed answered.

"The truth?"

"Yes, the truth."

"I didn't know your dad. Darla told me that he was a cop in another town and you two were in a witness protection program. I had just recovered from a gunshot wound and it was easiest to tell you and Oscar our lie." He rubbed his mouth with his napkin before putting it back in his lap. "Was he a cop in Whispering Falls?"

"From what I can gather, he was. And Darla left the village, but I'm not sure why." I didn't know anything about the witness protection program, but I was definitely putting that on my list of questions for the council after Jordan and I catch the killer. "How did you get Oscar?"

That was one question I had never asked before. I knew that his parents were killed in a car accident, but I never got the particulars.

"My older brother left for college and met a girl." There was sadness in his eyes. "She came to our house just one time. They eloped and we never saw them again. I didn't even know I had a nephew until my brother called telling me he was moving his family to Locust Grove. They got killed on the outskirts of town. Oscar was just a little fellow. I used all the department's resources to locate anyone in my brother's wife's family, but came up empty."

Sadness swept over me. No wonder there weren't any family photos in the house. "Oh, I'm so sorry. Does Oscar know?"

"Yes. I've always been very open about it." Regret dripped down his face. "I wished I knew my brother. There was not a will, nothing."

"I had no clue. I'm so sorry." I picked up Mr. Prince Charming. This was so much to take in with all the other stuff going on. A Ding Dong was calling my name. "I better get going."

I wasn't going to tell him that Oscar was a Fairiwick, because he obviously didn't know. Nor did he know about the voodoo dolls. Still, Eloise's words stung, "*He could be an evil spirit, but doesn't know it. I've seen a lot of little boys who make voodoo dolls that are spiritualist's and don't know it.*"

If that was the case, and I hated to think it, but the best friend that I've ever known or a stranger was on a mission to kill me. But why?

Chapter Twenty-Two

When I pulled out of Jordan's driveway, I carefully pulled out Madame Torres.

"You're back," sarcasm dripped in her voice. The globe was glowing a bright red.

"I am." I placed her between me and Mr. Prince Charming. "Are you going to show your face?"

"No." Her tongue was as sharp as a knife. "I wanted to help you."

I squeezed the steering wheel. "You can still help me."

"No, you ruined that. If you made a deal to buy me from Isadora Solstice I could've helped you." A couple of gold flashes and the globe went black again.

Hiss, hiss. Mr. Prince Charming batted at Madame Torres.

"She's testy." I patted Mr. Prince Charming. With or without Madame Torres help, I was going to find the killer and Jordan was going to help me.

Anxiously, I waited for midnight to come. I held off on calling Jordan to make sure he was going to be there. He affirmed that he would be, and there was no reason to believe otherwise. But it played in the back of my mind that he may have called Oscar and told him our plan.

I pulled the Green Machine on the outskirts of Whispering Falls behind some woods. I had to get to Eloise and tell her about my plan. If it didn't work out, and the killer got me and Jordan, at least someone would know what I was up to. Unfortunately I knew I couldn't share it with someone inside the village and that included Oscar.

"Okay, buddy." I put my bag over my shoulder and place Madame Torres inside. "You found Eloise's once. Can you find our way from this side of town?"

I took Mr. Prince Charming out of the car and put him on the ground. With his tail wagging in the air, he pranced off and I ran behind him.

It didn't take long until we reached a clearing. In the distance I could see the back of Eloise's tree house. As quickly as my legs would take me, I ran as fast as I could so no one would see me. If the village knew I was gone, they were probably looking for me.

The closer I got, the aromas of the cauldrons engrossed my senses.

"You've got to be kidding me?" Madame Torres chirped from my bag. "I'm a crystal ball, not a bouncy ball. Slow down!"

I ran faster.

"Eloise?" I yelled into the garden once I reached the gravel walkway. The lanterns burned bright. "Are you here?"

"June? Are you okay?" Eloise popped up from the Singing Pettles row and wiped her hands on her apron.

"Hmmm" The Singing Pettles had their leaves to the sun. "Laalaa."

I shook my head. "I'm never going to get use to this life."

Eloise put them in the basket on the ground with the other ones she had picked.

"I can only pick them once a week or they give me a headache with all that singing." She laughed and walked towards me. "You look frightened. Are you okay?"

"Okay?" A shadow of annoyance crossed my face. "You know I'm not okay." I stomped my foot.

"I'm not a toy!" Madame Torres screamed from my bag.

I opened it and stuck my face in it. "Shut up!" I snapped the flap down, and looked at Eloise. Tears streamed down my face. "I'm not okay! A couple of days ago I was just a girl with a quirky mom who sold fake homeopathic remedies at a flea market and was the most wonderful best friend in the world."

Eloise put her hands out for me to take.

I shook my head and walked backward a few steps. "No. I'm not okay," I said through gritted teeth. "Now I'm a girl that has some kind of power. I see people when they really aren't there. I have an angry crystal ball in my bag. My cat steals. Not only am I accused of being a murderer, I'm being framed. I don't know who or what I am!"

I fell to the ground with my head in my hands.

"Um. . .can you take it easy during your nervous breakdown?" Madame Torres' was muffled.

Eloise bent down and held me. She sat there with me while I cried. This entire situation had finally gotten to me.

"I shouldn't have run away." I took my purse off my shoulder and pulled Madame Torres out. I held her up to Eloise. "I stole this."

Eloise smiled. "Hi, Madame Torres."

The ball glowed the normal green. "Well, well. Look what June dragged in. Where in the world have you been?"

"Banned." Eloise took the ball, and then picked up the basket of Singing Pettles.

"I hate to break up this little reunion, but I need some help." I stood up and brushed the dirt off my clothes. I picked up my bag and put it back on my shoulder.

Eloise had a great idea. "Let's go have a Ding Dong." She continued her conversation with Madame Torres as I followed behind to the Gazebo.

Eloise sat Madame Torres on the table next to the Singing Pettles. They hummed away happily.

"Do you mind?" Madame Torres' eyes shot in the directions of the basket. "They give me a head-ache."

I couldn't help but smile as I ate my Ding Dong. Madame Torres was a pain-in-the-butt. Thank God she wasn't in human form.

"Tell me what is going on?" Eloise set the basket on the other side of the gazebo. They still let out a low hum, but nothing like before.

"I have a plan that I put into motion with Oscar's Uncle Jordan." I told Eloise how I was going to go to the lake because I had the nightmare about the next victim being me. "I wanted to tell you just in case it doesn't work out, and the killer kills me and Jordan."

Eloise wrung her hands as she paced back and forth. "I don't like this idea." She picked at her short red hair.

"I need some of that truth serum that you and Darla gave Izzy that time." If I could give some to the killer, which had to be one of the council members, including

Oscar, they'd sing like one of the Singling Pettles and confess to everything.

The heavy leashes that shadowed her cheeks flew up. "How did you know about that?"

"Darla's journal." I patted my bag.

"I don't think that would be a good idea. You never know what someone is going to say." She looked away.

Madame Torres' head went from one end of the globe to the other trying to keep up with our conversation.

"Eloise, I need you just like Darla needed you." I pleaded with her. She was a crucial part to ending this madness. "I have to hear them confess to murdering Ann and why. I fear that the answers to the death of my parents relies on the confession."

"I don't know." She spread her arms out in front of her and sprinkled hot pink dust into the air. The rows of plants bloomed to their fullest. The colors lit up the garden like a rainbow.

I took my phone out of my bag. "It's eleven o'clock. I have one hour until I meet Jordan."

"They are going to have my head if this backfires." She drew her arms in and pointed towards Whispering Falls. "They will come after me with burning torches."

"No. No they won't." This was going to work. If I was going to rely on my intuition like Darla told me to, everything was going to work out if everyone did what they were supposed to do.

Eloise's cloak swooshed around her as she drew her hands into the air. A clap of thunder rang out, but the stars in the sky were as bright as the day.

She rushed through the garden picking several different plants and flowers. She gathered them in her palm over the top of the cauldron. With one blow from her lips, the flowers turned into a pile of dust. She brushed them into the cauldron and stirred until it bubbled over.

"Hand me a bottle." She pointed toward the gazebo windowsill. "Anyone will be fine."

I grabbed the purple one with the star cap. It seemed the most appropriate.

Eloise took it from my hand and scooped up the overflow of the cauldron. She cast her eyes on me. "Use this with *extreme* caution. I suggest you take a bottle of water and add a couple of drops. Only a couple of drops." She wiggled her finger back and forth. She repeated, "Only a couple of drops."

Carefully I placed the bottle in my bag and grabbed a bottle of water from the table.

"Mr. Prince Charming, you stay here with Eloise and Madame Torres." I didn't want him to see if anything happened to me. I knew that Eloise would take care of him. "Please return Madame Torres if something goes wrong."

"No you won't. I'm not going back in some glass case or dark closet." The ball lit up bright red.

Eloise grabbed me by the shoulders and drew me close to her. "Keep safe sweet, sweet, June."

I held onto her words as I made my way into the dark night, through the woods and around the rock. I could see the lake as clear as day.

Chapter Twenty-Three

My heartbeat echoed so loudly that I was sure it could be heard all over Whispering Falls. Patiently I waited in the woods for Jordan's signal. I sat down in the grass and reached into my bag to get Darla's journal and my phone. I used the phone's keypad light to read a page in the journal.

"I thought Otto's job as a police officer was getting to him after he told me about the people that have come to visit him. He said someone was sitting next to June, but I didn't see anyone. I told Eloise about it and she didn't make me feel any better. She believes that Otto is a medium, which means that he's a Fairiwick. That would be devastating to him. He loves Whispering Falls and couldn't imagine being banned."

"Medium?" I whispered. Wasn't that when people saw dead people? Did my dad die because someone found out he was a Fairiwick?

What about me? Did that mean. . .I drew back and threw the journal in my bag. Had the mysterious shadow been a spirit? Was I part medium? Did the killer only want to kill off the Fairiwicks and found out who I was?

Freight and share agony pierced my soul. I was living someone's life, but not mine. . . not the one I knew. I grabbed my phone and stood up. It was ten after midnight and I hadn't seen Jordan's flashlight signal. Just when I was about to put my phone in my bag it vibrated.

"June, where are you?" The text from Oscar had a big red exclamation on it as though it was urgent. *"We need to talk."*

Talk? At midnight? Either they had the council meeting and he was going to put me in jail or he was looking for me because he was the killer.

I didn't respond. Either way, he'd find out where I was soon enough.

I'd give Jordan another ten minutes.

I unscrewed the cap off the bottle of water. I used the light from my phone so I could see what I was doing. Carefully I held it between my legs and took out the potion.

One, two. I counted the drips of the serum as it went into the water. I replaced the cap on the water and shook it up.

Off in the distance I saw a quick two flashes. Jordan was here. It was time. I wished I had a few more seconds so I could eat a Ding Dong. It might be the last time I tasted the delicious goodness.

Instead, I stood up with the water bottle in my hand and putting one foot carefully in front of the other, I walked towards the lake.

The ground became mushy the closer I got to the edge of the water. I couldn't help but wonder if this was how Ann felt before she took her last breath.

The lake was still, the water didn't move. It lay like glass. The moonbeams shone off the water into the clearing. The silence rang in my ears and the only thing I could feel was the beating of my heart.

I looked around to see if I could see anything. The fireflies played in the distance. They seemed to chase each other in circles and then in a straight line. Suddenly they darted into the night.

"We've been out here for about an hour." Jordan whispered.

"You scared me." I dropped the bottle. "Go back and hide. Let's give it a little while."

"Maybe you didn't see your nightmare right." He picked up the bottle.

I looked out onto the lake. I shook my head and recalled the vivid images from my nightmare. "No. It was my bracelet, I'm sure of it." I turned back around. "NO!" I screamed and smacked the water bottle from his lips.

"What? I'm thirsty." Jordan's eyes grew dark and he stepped backwards. "I think you are losing your mind."

Just like a spotlight, the moon shone down on the ground between us, exposing Jordan's footsteps in the soggy mud. It was the same shoe print I found where Ann was killed and under my window sill from the Cape Cod.

"Oh, no." I drew in my breath and put my hands up to my mouth. My intuition nagged me. "You killed Ann?"

"What? What did you say?" He ran toward me. His hand reached out as I tried to run.

The mud was like quicksand. I couldn't move. The harder I tried the more my feet dug into the marsh.

"Where do you think you are going, June?" He smiled, the evil showed in his eyes. He picked up the bottle and drank the rest of it before he crushed it in his grip. "Killing someone always makes me thirsty. But none of the others brought me a drink. Thank you." He threw the bottle in the lake.

None of the others? I only knew about Ann.

Like the water rippled from the effect, chills rippled throughout my body with each word that escaped from his lips. I tried to pull up a foot, but I was already buried to my calves.

"You psychics are all like. You think you can rule the world. Especially the Fairiwicks." He paced back and forth, not getting too close. He knew I was stuck. "Do you know what it's like being the outcast in a family, June?"

I shook my head. He drew a gun from underneath his shirt and waved it at me.

"My brother, my parent's, we were part of a village out west. We were all banned because I didn't have any powers. I was the runt." He jabbed himself with his gun. "Do you know what animals do with runts, June?"

"They get rid of them?" My voice quivered.

"Yes, June. They get rid of them. And that is what the *village* did to me. They got rid of *me*, making my family hate me. Shun me." He swayed the gun towards Whispering Falls. "And now I'm going to get rid of all of them."

"But Oscar and I love you." It was worth trying every emotional tactic I could to get him to let me go.

"You did, until you found out the truth." He plopped down in the grass with the gun pointed straight at me. "Your father heard I left the village out west from my brother and his crazy fairy wife. They came looking for me and I used my best magic on them." He held his gun up and dropped his head between his legs. "This gun is my magic."

A tear fell down my cheek. He had killed my father.

I reached down while he wasn't looking, dug in the mud and untied my shoes. The truth serum was setting in. He was spilling his guts. I slipped my hand into my bag and turned on the record button. He might kill me, but there was a chance that someone could find my phone.

I slipped the phone into the grass right before he looked up.

"It was priceless. They all came 'to talk,' but I knew better. They wanted to kill me." He stood up and came closer. He held the gun to his chest. The mole between his thumb and finger was exactly like the one from my nightmare. I knew what fate had in store for me.

"The fat one, Ann, she was Oscar's nanny. She ran and I couldn't find her. I had no idea where Whispering Falls was until dear sweet Oscar wanted to move here."

"Did you kill my mother?" I had to ask before he killed me. She was so young to die of a heart attack.

"Darla. Beautiful Darla." His fists clinched. "I had no idea who she was when you moved into Locust Grove. By the time she moved in, Oscar was settled. He had so much promise."

"What do you mean?"

"I thought he was like me. You know. . .the runt."

"I had no intentions of hurting anyone else until Darla found my little box of voodoo dolls."

I gasped. All this time I thought it was Oscar who made them.

"What? Do you think I could let her live after she knew exactly what they were?" He threw his head back and laughed. "I let her live until you were older, then you could take care of yourself. So I watched you mix all those remedies, only you could never get them right. I figured you could live because you weren't a crazy one. And Oscar is too dumb to be a police officer so when he wanted to move here, I let him."

"Seeing Ann was icing on the cake. So I stole your charm bracelet because we both know you sleep heavy when you are dreaming and after I killed her, I put your bracelet in her hand."

"It was all too easy. I made sure everything was done at night so no one saw me."

He was wrong! My eyes darted back and forth looking for the fireflies. Of all nights the teenagers decided to go to bed early? They were nowhere to be found.

"That smudging thing with Gerald was priceless." His laughter rang out. "I didn't have a hand in that, but that was great."

"I'm glad you find it amusing." The adrenaline rushed through my body. I tapped my leg with my fingertips. There had to be a good time to run. "Why me? What did I do to you? Are you going to kill Oscar?"

His breathing deepened. His jaw line flexed and became rigid, as he chose his words carefully. "Oscar is dumb. If he did have powers, which he doesn't, he would screw it up. You..." he pointed the gun towards me again, "you are a smart one. Without you around, I can keep Oscar. He won't last long here. Especially after I pick them off one-by-one."

He was crazy if he didn't think one of the spiritualists was going to figure out it was him. And to think that I thought Gerald or Oscar had something to do with this.

Jordan put his gun back in the waist of his pants and slowly walked towards me. "It's time, June. Now you be a good girl."

I jumped out of my shoes and ran. His footsteps were thunderous behind me.

"Help! Help me!" I screamed into the night air. I felt his hands grab at me. I flung my wrist when I felt his touch. My bracelet snapped and flew into the lake. Without hesitation I ran faster, but not fast enough.

Ouch! I crumbled to the ground as Jordan grabbed a handful of my hair. He thrust my helpless body to the edge of the lake and in one swoop he had my head under water just like my nightmare, only this time I was *living it*.

I reached behind me smacking the air hoping I would make contact, but come up with air every time. I grabbed his hands that were holding me underneath. My nightmare played in my head as I flailed about. Something was different. I didn't have on the bracelet on like I did in my nightmare.

I flailed more, kicking my legs. With every kick, my head bobbled above the water. I gasped for more air. Just as I was about to give up, I felt a rough tongue on my foot, and then Jordan's hands released me.

Without looking, I dragged myself out of the water and gulped for air.

Hiss, hissssss. Mr. Prince Charming had jumped up on Jordan's back and stuck to him like glue. Jordan was running in circles trying to get him off.

"Get him!" The glowing green ball from afar was making its way across the meadow. The moonlight shown on Eloise and Madame Torres.

"He has a gun!" I mustered up every ounce of energy in my body.

Eloise sat Madame Torres on the ground. A clap of thunder rolled over Whispering Falls as Eloise drew her hands together and blew. Lime green dust shot like a bee out of her hands and into Jordan's eyes.

He let out a blood-curdling scream and fell to the ground.

"Over here!" Petunia called out into the darkness. I watched as the fireflies led the pack of spiritualists.

They did go for help. The teenagers went to get help.

"Oh my God. June?" Oscar ran over to me and brushed my wet bangs out of my eyes. He glanced over at Jordan who appeared lifeless just a few feet away.

"My phone." I pointed in the direction of where it was. "Get my phone."

Oscar reached into the deep brush and got the phone. He handed it to me before he saw Jordan lying in the thicket.

"Oh my God, Uncle Jordan?" Oscar ran to his side. "What happened?"

Oscar grabbed Uncle Jordan and placed him in his lap. Streaks of light shot from his eyes, "What did you do?" He glared at me.

"I didn't do anything. He is the killer! He has a gun!" I screamed, and pushed the button on my phone to play back everything that happened.

Jordan's words twisted and curled into the night air. He sat with his shoulders slumped, completely silent.

I looked around at Izzy, Gerald, Petunia, Chandra, and Oscar as the recording rang in the dark. Jordan was only able to move his eyes. They darted from side to side.

"You killed my parents?" Oscar pulled the gun from Jordan's waistband, and jumped to his feet. His anger became a raging fury. "I should kill you with my bare hands!"

"No." I stood up next to Oscar and put my hand on his bicep. "You are better than him. Ann was your nanny. You are a spiritualist. Eloise put some kind of spell on Jordan. He can't move."

Out of the moon's shadow and into the light, Eloise appeared with Madame Torres in her hand.

"Eloise is your aunt." I gestured for her to come forward. I took Madame Torres from her.

A little hesitant from all of the stares, she enclosed Oscar in her cloak. "I can't wait to tell you all about your mom and dad," she whispered in his ear.

Mr. Prince Charming danced around their ankles.

Chapter Twenty-Four

The day was dawning.

The Karmina sister's hearse barreled up the hill. The lights flashed, lighting up the starry sky. Constance jumped out, velcro curlers all over her hair. "Who's next?" She shined a flashlight in everyone's face.

Patience wasn't too far behind. "Who's next?" she chirped and shuffled over in her pink house slippers. She picked up a stick and poked Jordan. "He's a fresh one."

Jordan jerked his shoulders back and glared at Patience. "Don't poke the bear or he just might bite."

Patience jumped and held the stick like a gun. "He's not dead."

"I'll get you all!" Jordan scowled as Oscar cuffed him. Oscar jerked him up by the cuffs and hauled him off to the police station.

Eloise started to slip out of the daylight and into the woods, but Izzy stopped her.

"Wait, Eloise." Izzy turned to the council. "Come have some tea at the Gathering Grove."

With Eloise smiling, we all walked in silence with Mr. Prince Charming trotting ahead.

Bella and Axelrod had the tea and muffins ready when we got there. Oscar joined us once he got Jordan situated in his cell.

"I'm so sorry, June." Oscar sat in the seat next to me. He took my wrist and clasped my turtle charm bracelet around it. "We will drag the lake and look for your other one."

I opened my bag and pulled out two Ding Dongs. I handed him one. "You're forgiven."

"How did you find my aunt?" His eyes clouded over. It was the first time I had ever seen Oscar brought to tears.

"Hold on a second." I stood up on the chair to gather everyone's attention. "I have something to say."

The Gathering Grove became silent. Everyone looked at me.

"There are a lot of rules in this village. And a lot I have to learn. Eloise saved us today. She and Ann were banned from Whispering Falls because they are Fairiwicks. I think it's time that the village changes the rules to include anyone in the spiritual realm. We are much better as a collective whole than apart. Eloise has so much to offer our village with her potions. Without the truth serum, Jordan probably wouldn't have spilled the beans and I would be dead." Mr. Prince Charming caught my eye as he danced around the table where Petunia was sitting. I tried to concentrate on what I was saying, but I couldn't. Petunia was whispering in his ear.

"I. . ..um. . ." *Snap out of it, there was no way Mr. Prince Charming was. . .oh my God!* "I . . .I would like to take a vote at the next village meeting to incorporate the Fairiwicks into the Whispering Falls village."

A round of applause rang out. Even Izzy got up and hugged Eloise, but this was going to have to go through Oscar. He wasn't letting go.

Gerald and Petunia were behind the counter making sure everyone had what they needed.

"Gerald, remember when you were reading my tea leaves?" There were some things he had mentioned that I didn't understand.

He nodded and handed a muffin over the counter to Oscar.

"What did my reading say?" I asked.

"Are you giving me permission to tell you from one spiritualist to another?"

"Yes." No matter what my leaves said, I still wanted to know.

He took his hat off and placed it on top the counter. He leaned over and proceeded with a low whisper, "The O represented your father, Otto. He is always with you. As is your grandfather."

Mr. Prince Charming jumped up on the counter.

"No. That's naughty." I scolded him and put him back on the ground. He might be able to jump up on the counters at home, but not here. "Go on."

"The wavy lines told me you were in for a rocky future. Which I don't believe is over." He drew back, took in a deep breath, and closed his eyes. "Madame Torres had warned the village of a powerful psychic coming to town and that her nightmares would prove innocence." His shoulders slumped a little bit.

"Are you okay?" I reached over the counter to pat his hand.

Petunia grabbed a chair and eased him into it. "He gets this way when he reads the leaves. Sometimes the spirit takes over."

Cough, cough. "I'm fine." Gerald held his fist to his mouth. "You are on a path to discovering your gifts. Don't limit yourself." He stood up. "I must get some rest now."

Without another word, Gerald went to the back of the shop.

"That was weird," I said to Oscar and shrugged my shoulders. "Let's go sit."

Oscar nabbed the closest table and sat down. He pointed to himself. "I'm a sorcerer."

"No, you are a police officer." I could feel the excited, renewed energy he had. "You worry about keeping our village safe."

"I think it's cool. According to Eloise, I will begin my lessons soon with the new Fairiwicks moving into town." His features became more animated. He acted like he was a kid at Christmas.

"They already heard that Whispering Falls is going to make it official at the next council meeting?" I looked over at Eloise and Izzy.

"It doesn't take long for a spiritualist to listen to the winds." Izzy smiled.

I pulled Eloise aside. I was still having a hard time and questioning my entire existence. "Was my dad a medium?" My eyes darted between her eyes searching for an answer.

The shadowy figure could have been Jordan watching me all this time, or it could be a spirit.

"Darla and I never made it that far." Eloise took both my hands. "She asked me about it hours before he was found dead. Why?"

"She wrote something about it in the journal." I wasn't going to tell her that I had seen a shadow or two. There was no need to jump to any conclusion. I had plenty of time to explore my village. Today was for celebrating.

"So, do you love us or what?" Bella smiled and hugged me. "You realize you own the cottage you are living in."

"Patience kind of let the cat out of the bag." Even though I didn't remember it from my childhood, the cottage did feel like home.

"Darla always knew you'd find out, but we had hoped she would've shared the experience with you." Bella wiped a tear from her eye. "Welcome home."

We embraced.

There was a lot to learn about Whispering Falls. There was a lot to learn about being a spiritualist. And I had the rest of my life to do it.

I opened my bag and took out Darla's journal and rubbed my hands across the beat up leather cover. I took a good long look around the Gathering Grove. My first few days in Whispering Falls had been rocky, at best, but each one of these people held a special bond. They were a part of me. They were a part of my past. And I was embracing who I really was.

I held the journal close to my heart. My instincts told me there was a lot in there to learn, and I couldn't wait to savor every word.

Quietly, Mr. Prince Charming and I headed to our cottage. Once we reached our front door, we turned around and looked over Whispering Falls.

Mewl, mewl. His long white tail danced in the air.

I looked down at the ornery cat. He dropped something out of his mouth. I bent down to pick it up. He did figure eights around my ankles.

I held the small charm in the palm of my hand. "Mr. Prince Charming, what does this mean?" I dangled the metal, in the shape of a hand, in the air to get a good look.

I made a mental note to visit Bella in the morning to return it. I was too tired to even think about opening the shop. Besides, it was my shop now and I needed to have the sign redone for the grand opening of Charming Cures.

After all, there was going to be a big line of customers and I had to be ready for them. At least that was what my intuition told me.

About The Author

International bestselling author Tonya Kappes believes that targeted and smart promotion and marketing can take a book from lackluster sales to the world of bestseller. She pooled her resources and knowledge to write The Tricked Out Toolbox: Promotion and Marketing Tools Every Writer Needs. When not touting marketing and promotion through her workshops, she writes cozy mysteries, romantic suspense, and women's fiction. She's addicted to coffee, McDonald's Diet Coke, and Red Hots Candy!

When she's not writing about quirky characters and even quirkier situations, she's busy being the princess, queen and jester of her domain which includes her BFF husband, her four teenage boys and two dogs.

For more information, check out Tonya's website, Tonyakappes.blogspot.com.

Made in the USA
Middletown, DE
19 November 2019